Praise for Richard T. Ryan's Sherlock Holmes
Adventures

The Vatican Cameos

Winner of the Underground Book Reviews' "Novel of the
Year" Award. Winner Silver Medal in the Readers'
Favorite book-award contest.

"[*The Vatican Cameos* is] an extravagantly imagined and
beautifully written Holmes story." – Lee Child, NY Times
Bestselling author and the creator of Jack Reacher

"A great addition to the Holmes Canon. Definitely worth a
read." – Rob Hart, author of *The Warehouse* and the Ash
McKenna series

"*The Vatican Cameos* opens with a familiar feel for fans of
Arthur Conan Doyle's original Sherlock Holmes stories.
The plotting is clever, and the alternating stories well-told."
– Crime Thriller Hound

I0607505

The Stone of Destiny

"Sometimes a book comes along that absolutely restores your faith in reading. Such is the 'found manuscript' of Dr. Watson, *The Stone of Destiny*. Exhilarating, superb narrative and a cast of characters that are as dark as they are vivid. ... A thriller of the very first rank." – Ken Bruen, author of *The Guards, The Magdalen Martyrs,* and many other novels, as well as the creator of the Jack Taylor series

"A wonderful read for both the casual Sherlock Holmes fan and the most die-hard devotees of the beloved character." – Terrence McCauley, author of *A Conspiracy of Ravens* and *A Murder of Crows*

"Somewhere Sir Arthur Conan Doyle is smiling. Ryan's *The Stone of Destiny* is a fine addition to the Canon." – Reed Farrel Coleman, NY Times Bestselling author of *What You Break*

"Richard Ryan's prose flows as easily as a stream in the summer. I thought the way the Stone was stolen, how it was transported out of England under the very noses of the army of police, and its hiding place in Ireland were brilliant!" – Raven Reviews

"The clever solution, which echoes one from a golden age classic, is the book's best feature." – Publishers Weekly

"… the Druidic detail and the depiction of 19th-century London are fascinating and delightful." – Kirkus Reviews

"As one would expect from a Sherlock Holmes story, the Great Detective's intellect, keen eye for observation, and logical deductions all play a factor in the satisfying conclusion of this mystery." – Kristopher Zgorski, founder of BOLO Books

"Sherlockians craving a new challenge for their favorite sleuth need look no further than Richard T. Ryan's *The Druid of Death*, which puts Holmes on the trail of one of his most fiendish adversaries ever." – Steven Hockensmith, author of the Edgar Award finalist *Holmes on the Range*

"Oh, what a joy it is to meet Sherlock Holmes and Dr. Watson again! *The Merchant of Menace* is an exciting adventure of priceless valuables, great detective work and just the kind of devilish adversary we love to read about." – Mattias Boström, author of *From Holmes to Sherlock: The Story of the Men and Women Who Created an Icon*

"This rousing, intriguing, devilishly fun caper, well-executed and well-paced, had me hooked from the first page. The dutiful Watson, Holmes' deductive skills, and a worthy nemesis to rival the evil Moriarty himself, make this cat-and-mouse adventure a page-turning, edge-of-your-seat roller-coaster ride well worth taking." – Tracy Clark, author of *Broken Places* and *Borrowed Time* and the creator of Cass Raines

"[*The Merchant of Menace* is] an absolute humdinger of a novel ...It is beautifully written, erudite and hugely entertaining." – Ken Bruen, the author of *The Ghosts of Galway* and the creator of Jack Taylor

"With an intriguing premise and a cunning plot, *The Merchant of Menace* will delight Sherlockians of all stripes. Richard T. Ryan has given us a gripping mystery and a loving tribute to the Great Detective." – Daniel Stashower, author of *Teller of Tales: The Life of Arthur Conan Doyle*

"Deftly blending Conan Doyle and Dan Brown, Richard Ryan's *Through a Glass Starkly* offers an intriguing mix of history and mystery. Remaining true to the Canon in his depictions of the iconic Holmes and Watson, Ryan also delivers a mystery that should satisfy even the most demanding Sherlockian." – Robert Dugoni, NY Times Bestselling author of *The Eighth Sister* and the creator of Tracy Crosswhite

"Ryan's Watsonian voice is superb, and as with his earlier novels the author has included several affectionate nods to the characters, stories, and intrigues of the original Canon. These twists and turns make this an engrossing and enjoyable read, as do the variety of colourful locations chosen for the action. From a secret *pied-a-terre* in Paris, to the Whispering Gallery in St. Paul's Cathedral, we are carried along at a frenetic pace. I previously read, and thoroughly enjoyed, *The Druid of Death*. *Through a Glass Starkly* is even better!" – Sherlock Holmes Society of London

"Another brilliant addition to the Sherlock Holmes Canon." – Bruce Robert Coffin, author of the Detective Byron mysteries

"Slap on your deerstalker and grab a pipe, Richard Ryan's Sherlock Holmes strikes again. With head-scratching twists and puzzling turns, even Arthur Conan Doyle would be hard-pressed to solve this mystery. *Through a Glass Starkly* will satisfy even the most ardent Holmes fans." – Jean M. Roberts @thebookdelight.com and author of *The Heron*

Three May Keep a Secret

"Richard T. Ryan's *Three May Keep a Secret* [is] a pitch-perfect adventure that pits Conan Doyle's great detective against a master criminal…It's a tale of fabulous jewels, brilliant forgeries, cunning disguises and a Watson double-act that will make every writer who's ever penned a Holmes pastiche green with 'Why didn't I think of that?'" – Jeffrey Hatcher, screenwriter for *Mr. Holmes*

"Richard Ryan has yet again given us one of his well-crafted yet exciting and entertaining novels of Sherlock Holmes. Settle in for several hours of fun reading." – Robert Katz, MD, BSI

"… the book's strengths, including the imaginative setup, make Ryan's taking up Conan Doyle's mantle again welcome. Fans of traditional pastiches will enjoy this." – Publishers Weekly

"The tour de force in the book is the presence of a criminal mastermind, a worthy replacement for Professor Moriarty, whose shadows are broodingly present in the adventure." – *Sherlock Holmes Society of India*

The Poisoned Pawn

"Richard Ryan has again penned another fast paced and carefully plotted pastiche. The characterizations are both strong and canonical. The story is replete with the requisite twists and turns, intriguing villains, and surprise endings. It moves quickly, establishes the necessary atmosphere, and maintains the quality that he's long developed." – Robert Katz, MD, BSI

"An absorbing narrative with a devilish plot – top marks for Richard T. Ryan's latest novel which captures the true spirit of Conan Doyle." – Mark Mower, author of *Sherlock Holmes: The Baker Street Archive*

"It's indeed a pleasure to read a novel in which Professor Moriarty is pulling the strings of another criminal from behind the scenes. In *The Poisoned Pawn*, Richard T. Ryan has the professor maneuver a villain seeking personal revenge into a deadly game against Sherlock Holmes. A rousing adventure from start to finish!" — Ray Riethmeier, editor of *Sherlock Holmes: Stranger Than Truth* and *Sherlock Holmes: Stranger Than Fiction*

"Fans of Sherlock Holmes, both young and older, will enjoy Richard T. Ryan's entertaining tale of *The Poisoned Pawn* from chapter to chapter, anxiously awaiting for what comes next! Very well-researched and detailed! Sit back and enjoy!" – Greg D. Ruby, BSI, ASH, The SOB in Charge The Sherlockians of Baltimore

The Traitorous Templar:
A Sherlock Holmes Adventure

by Richard T. Ryan

Hardcover ISBN 978-1-80424-502-6
Paperback ISBN 978-1-80424-503-3
AUK ePub 978-1-80424-504-0
AUK PDF 978-1-80424-505-7

Published by MX Publishing
335 Princess Park Manor, Royal Drive, London, N11 3GX
www.mxpublishing.com

Cover design by Brian Belanger

This book is dedicated to three very special little people:

Brody Edward, Henry Robert and Riley Grace.

As always, it is also dedicated to my wife, Grace.

"The greatest battle is not fought with swords,
but within the depths of one's own soul."

— Attributed to a member of the Knights Templar

"Let evil swiftly befall those who have wrongly
condemned us – God will avenge us."

– Jacques de Molay,
last Grandmaster
of the Templars

"It is, of course, a trifle, but there is
nothing so important
as trifles."

– Sherlock Holmes,
"The
Adventure of the Twisted Lip"

Foreword

Of the many strange tales featuring Sherlock Holmes and Dr. Watson, which were contained in a tin dispatch box I won at an estate auction at St. Andrew's in Scotland, there is a certain singularity about this specific recollection that makes it worthy of consideration.

As I have indicated in the past, certain stories which I have brought to light were apparently withheld for political reasons, others because of reticence on the part of either Holmes or Watson or both. However, I can find no overt reason for Watson's decision to consign this particular adventure to the tin box rather than his publisher.

That said, the first thing that struck me after I plucked this particular sheaf of papers from the chest was the title page. Although the title *The Traitorous Templar* had been written in ink on the third page of the manuscript, right above Dr. Watson's introduction, the cover page bore the legend – *The Arrest of Wilson, the Notorious Canary Trainer*. As a result, I was led to believe that I was going to read one of the many untold tales mentioned in the Canon.

In the case of Wilson, to whom Watson had alluded in "Black Peter," he added that canary trainer's arrest had "removed a plague-spot from the East End of London."

However, it was obvious after just a few pages, not counting the introduction which only added to my confusion, that this was not the case. Although I still long to know more about Wilson, this adventure, involving the Knights Templar rather than an infamous avian instructor, proved quite satisfying. As a result, whatever slight misgivings I may have harbored initially soon gave way to feelings of an entirely different nature. I have no idea why this adventure was mistitled and I remain even more puzzled as to why it was withheld from publication.

There is nothing politically sensitive nor overtly offensive as near as I can tell. At first I had thought the tale might be some sort of *roman à clef,* but I was soon disabused of that notion.

So, what we end up with is a riddle wrapped in a mystery. There is no enigma involved – or at least not one that I can see. Why was the manuscript bound with an incorrect title page and why has it never seen the light of day until now?

My guess (Holmes would have hated those words) is that we shall probably never know. However, had I answers to one or both, you may rest assured that I would certainly share them with you; unfortunately, the best that I can offer by way of explanation is this manuscript which others may be able to interpret to their own satisfaction. I would be interested to learn at what conclusions others may arrive.

Richard T. Ryan, March 13, 2024

Introduction

Several years have now passed since Holmes and I found ourselves involved in one of the strangest adventures in my friend's long and distinguished career. During that time, he has been of assistance to kings and queens as well as scullery maids and hansom drivers. For him the case has always been of primary importance – far more so than any notoriety or monetary recompense he might have received by choosing to involve himself.

At the time of the case, I took copious notes and diligently recorded them in my journals. However, that was such a busy period that I never did get around to organizing them until more than half a decade had passed.

Like so many other of his cases, this one began in a fairly innocuous manner. The events were not precipitated by anything as frightening as the revelation of the presence of "the footprints of a giant hound." Rather, things were set in motion by the appearance of some wayward tallow droppings on the floor of a nearby art gallery.

As you might expect, Holmes was intrigued when presented with the situation, and as you also might expect, once he had picked up the scent he was like a relentless hound.

As a result, we traveled to the village of Roystan and subsequently to various locales in and around Cornwall. At each stop along the way, Holmes found himself presented with an array of clues – as well as a few red herrings – the significance of which I am certain would have eluded a lesser intellect.

During our excursions we were confronted by formidable adversaries; we also received assistance from some invaluable allies. On more than one occasion, our lives were in imminent danger. Despite the obstacles, Holmes persevered and in the end, he triumphed where I am certain so many others might have thrown in the towel and resigned themselves to defeat. After all, who would have known?

Obviously Holmes would have known and while he could accept the occasional failure, that acceptance came only after he had expended every effort to secure the victory for his client – and by extension, himself.

Having said that, Holmes pursued this case with the same purpose that he brought to bear on all such endeavours. The result, though satisfying in some way, did little to burnish his reputation, and he earned no great fee at the end of it, despite the tremendous sums involved.

No, I am afraid this case is little more than an example of Holmes's patience and brilliance as well as his willingness to follow a trifle to the ends of the earth. To do otherwise would have been anathema to his disciplined spirit.

Having said that, dear reader, I offer for your consideration *The Adventure of the Traitorous Templar.*

Dr. John H. Watson

13 March, 1902

Chapter 1

Peace and tranquility were repugnant to Sherlock Holmes. So after five days had passed without a case to break the monotony, my flatmate had become rather irascible. Having foresworn the needle, Sherlock Holmes had decided to while away an hour or two by indulging in one of his favourite pastimes. He would position himself at the window overlooking Baker Street and stand there for hours. From that vantage point, he could watch the comings and goings of the throngs traversing the thoroughfare below. He would then select some passerby, who had caught his attention, and begin to analyse that individual's dress, gait, complexion and other pertinent characteristics in an effort to ascertain the person's occupation and the business that had brought him or her hither. Although his deductions often went untested, on those occasions when they were scrutinised, he was, as you might expect, seldom wrong regarding the conclusions at which he had arrived.

I was reading the paper that fine spring morning in 1895, when my thoughts were suddenly interrupted as Holmes broke the silence, exclaiming, "Halloa! What have we here? A fine Clarence with matching stallions. The driver is obviously looking for a house number – and he appears to have found it." After a few seconds he turned to me and said, "Unless I am very much mistaken, a new client – one with whom I have some slight acquaintance – has come to seek our assistance."

Doffing his dressing gown and donning his frock coat, Holmes then proceeded to collect several piles of papers that had been strewn about the floor; after casting about the room, he decided to conceal them by shoving them down behind the settee. Well aware of how totally unconcerned with appearances Holmes was as a rule, I thought, "This must be some dignitary or potentate. After all, Sherlock Holmes doesn't tidy up the flat for just anyone."

A minute or two later, I heard the doorbell ring, and shortly after that, Mrs. Hudson knocked on the door. "Come in, Mrs. Hudson," said Holmes.

Our landlady entered and said, "A gentleman is here to see you, sir." After handing Holmes the man's card, she offered, "He says it is a matter of some urgency, sir."

"Please show him up, dear lady. And if you would be so kind, perhaps you might bring up a pot of tea and possibly a few biscuits if any are available."

I was rather taken aback at Holmes's courtliness and began to wonder who this visitor might be. Fortunately, I hadn't long to wait as just a moment later, a prosperous-looking man in his late-fifties or early sixties tentatively knocked on the open door. He was of medium height and build with brown hair and a full moustache. He wore a light grey suit with a starched white shirt and an understated maroon cravat. He seemed altogether an unprepossessing individual which made Holmes's actions seem that much stranger.

"Come in," said Holmes. "Please take a seat," he said indicating one of the wing chairs by the hearth.

"I do hope I haven't come at an inopportune time, Mr. Holmes," he said, "but the matter is most pressing – at least to me." Having made this pronouncement, he sat and fidgeted as he waited for Holmes to speak.

After a few seconds when Holmes remained silent, he began, "My name is Paul Rotondo and I serve as the ..."

Holmes cut him off, "I am well aware of who you are, sir, and of your position as head curator with the Wallace Collection. I also know you keep a small brindle terrier, prefer marmalade jam and enjoy painting landscapes as a hobby."

Rotondo looked astounded at Holmes' pronouncements, but I had seen those tricks before. Looking closer, I could discern a slight smudge of jam on the outside of his left cuff and the dark dog hair stood out against the cuffs of his light grey trousers, but how Holmes had arrived at the painting escaped me. Looking up, I saw Holmes watching me, and he smiled ever so slightly.

"Still, you didn't come here to discuss your personal life, so what has upset you to the point that you feel as though you require my assistance?"

"Since you know who I am, I can only assume you have visited the collection since it is so close by."

"Indeed, I have been there on a number of occasions – usually for research with regard to a case, but now and then for pleasure. I am quite fond of Franz Hals's *The Laughing Cavalier,* but again, you haven't come here to discuss my predilection for the Dutch masters either. So how may I be of assistance?"

Having regained his composure, Rotondo began again, "As you know, the Wallace Collection has a rather extensive display of arms and armour, dating from the medieval period up to and including the present day."

"Indeed, I once had occasion to borrow a 12th-century broadsword from the Collection, but that was some time ago before it was bequeathed to the nation and subsequently opened as a museum."

"And that's the strangest part of it, Mr. Holmes."

"Of what, exactly?" asked Holmes.

"The break-ins. As you have observed, the collection is now open to the public, yet I am quite certain that we are being frequented by a nocturnal visitor who surreptitiously has sneaked into the collection on a number of occasions – long after we have closed."

"As far as you know, has anything been taken?"

"To the best of my knowledge, nothing and that's what makes it so strange. For the most part, everything appears exactly as it was when we closed the previous evening."

"Let us start at the beginning. When did you first decide the collection was entertaining an untimely guest?"

"Suspicions were first raised perhaps a month ago. One of the docents discovered tallow drippings in front of a display of swords and shields in the first of the European Armoury rooms."

"If memory serves there are three rooms in which European weapons and armour are displayed and a fourth in which Oriental arms are emphasized."

"Quite right, Mr. Holmes, quite right. The first time anyone noticed the drippings was in that first armoury room which is located near the rear of Hertford House. Perhaps a week later, more droppings were found in the same room which is dedicated to Medieval and Renaissance Arms and Armour. The pieces in that section date from the 10th to the 16th centuries. Several days later, we discovered a similar scenario in the second European room, but both the third European room and the Oriental Armory appear to have been spared. Then a week after that our visitor apparently returned on two different nights to the medieval room."

"When did all this begin?" I asked.

"It was the third or fourth week in April, if memory serves," Rotondo replied.

"And how many times can you say for certain this visitor has sneaked into the collection?" asked Holmes, anticipating my next question.

"At least five times – on each visit he appears to have dripped tallow from either a candle or a dark lantern, and on the most recent occasion, while there was tallow, the intruder appears also to have left behind a small coin."

"The tallow droppings, where exactly were they in the room?" Holmes asked.

"On all but that one occasion, they were found on the floor near one of the cases containing a display of medieval armour. However, on the next to last visit perhaps a week ago, they were discovered in two different places in the same room. Some of the tallow was near a case holding shields and the other droppings were discovered near a case displaying various swords," replied Rotondo.

"And the coin? Where was it and what can you tell me about it?"

"That's the most unusual part of this whole thing," exclaimed Rotondo.

"Please elaborate," said Holmes.

"Like the most recent tallow splatters, the coin was discovered early this morning, which is why I am here. A member of the maintenance crew who was dusting the exhibits prior to opening came across it on a shelf in one of the display cases in the medieval armour room."

"Did you say it was discovered *in* a display case – not in front of it?"

"Yes, sir. The coin was locked inside along with the swords and shields."

"You are certain the case was locked?"

"It was."

"Is it possible the coin was dropped on one of the earlier visits and simply not discovered until this morning?"

"It is certainly possible but most unlikely, I think, as the items are dusted regularly, and the coin is shiny enough that I am certain it would have been spotted."

"So on four out of five occasions, the intruder appears to have spent time in the first European Armour room. Obviously, there is something there that seems to have captured and held his attention."

"Did you bring the coin with you?"

"No, I had the worker replace it in the exact spot where he discovered it."

"Bravo!" exclaimed Holmes. "I should very much like to examine that room although I will tell you now I am not optimistic," said Holmes.

"Because of the visitors?" I inquired.

"Exactly," replied my friend.

"Well, you needn't worry about that, Mr. Holmes. I closed the room to the public before the museum opened. You see," he said proudly, "I am somewhat familiar with your preferences and methods." With that, he gave me a knowing look and handed Holmes an envelope.

"What is this?" inquired Holmes, looking at the envelope.

"That is a sample of the droppings. I thought you might be able to glean something from them, so I scraped some off the floor and placed them in this envelope."

"Excellent!" exclaimed Holmes, smiling at the man. I very much fear you have missed your vocation, Mr. Rotondo. Would that Scotland Yard took as much care to preserve a crime scene as you appear to have done."

"Are you certain there has been a crime?" I asked.

"At the very least, we appear to have several occasions of breaking and entering. What other charges may be added to those remains to be seen. Mr. Rotondo, may I ask why you waited so long to contact me?"

"Since nothing appeared to have been taken, I just thought one of the workers had been careless and was lying about the drippings."

"Ah, I see," replied Holmes. Then ever the man of action, he looked at me and said, "Now, Watson, if you have nothing else to occupy your day, let us make haste to the Wallace Collection."

"My carriage is waiting downstairs, gentlemen," said Rotondo. And so it was that a few minutes later the three of us were headed toward Manchester Square. After the short ride, we entered through the rear of the building. As we did so, Rotondo explained that the European Armour was housed in what had once been the stables.

The doors to the room had been cordoned off and a small velvet rope stood before it with a sign proclaiming, "Closed for Renovations."

Rotondo took out a key and opened the doors. As soon as we entered, I was struck by the sheer number of weapons and suits of armour on display. In the middle of the room were several large cases filled with helms, gauntlets, swords, shields, dirks and other paraphernalia. Each case had been divided in half from side to side so that visitors could view different items depending upon which side they chose to examine first.

The walls on all sides of the room contained even more display cases while in between the cases shields displaying the coats of arms of some of the great families of England had been hung. The taller cases, though not as broad, housed entire suits of armour with various accoutrements while a number of the larger ones seemed to be dedicated to specific weapons and pieces of armour. One contained an astonishing array of broadswords and gauntlets while another featured a selection of breastplates, knives, maces and other menacing-looking weapons. A third was filled with an array of helms – the variety of which I found stunning.

Holmes and I followed Rotondo to one of the cabinets in the middle displaying swords and shields. After selecting a second key from his ring, Rotondo was about to open the cabinet when Holmes stopped him. "The coin was found inside the cabinet, you said," he stated.

"Indeed, that's what makes it so strange. Had it been found on the floor, it might not have been given a second thought but when the worker moved one of the shields to dust it, he discovered it laying behind it on the shelf."

"And you're certain it wasn't there before?"

"Indeed, Mr. Holmes. I had but a moment to examine it, but it appears to be quite old." He then turned to open the cabinet, but Holmes asked him to wait a moment. He then knelt on the floor in front of the lock and pulling his lens from his pocket began to examine it in some detail. "There appear to be fresh scratches," he said almost to himself.

After a few moments, he stood and turning to Rotondo, said, "Now, if you would, please open the cabinet."

Rotondo did as he was bade and pulled back a wide glass door.

"Behind which shield was it found?" asked Holmes.

The curator pointed to a partially hidden badge shield that was almost entirely obscured by a larger round shield. Rotondo removed the larger of the two, and we could see that the smaller badge shield had been divided into quarters. The upper left and lower right featured a red cross against a white background. (I later learned that in heraldry red is referred to as "gules.") The other two quarters sported gold bands running diagonally, from the upper left to the lower right, against a background of blue or azure.

"Have you any idea of the provenance of this shield?" asked Holmes.

"I believe it was acquired by Sir Richard Wallace in 1871, when he bought the collections of the Comte Alfred Emilien de Nieuwekerke, Minister of Fine Arts to Napoleon III and director of the Louvre. At the same time, Sir Richard also purchased the finest parts of the collection of Sir Samuel Rush Meyrick, a pioneering collector and scholar of arms and armour. I can only assume that's when it was acquired."

"Yes, yes, I'm sure that's all very interesting to scholars and academics," said Holmes with just a hint of impatience. "At present, the only part that intrigues me is that it appears the shield quite possibly came from France and may have been crafted in the late 13th or early 14th century."

"Is that important, Holmes?" I asked.

"Perhaps. Beyond its acquisition, can you provide any further information about the shield?"

"I'm afraid not, Mr. Holmes. My area of expertise is late-17th and early-18th century French furniture with a particular emphasis upon the work of André-Charles Boulle."

Turning to me, Holmes rolled his eyes and while he found the answer annoying, he remained cordial when he said to Rotondo, "So beyond what you have told us, you know nothing else about the shield?"

"I wish I could be of more help, Mr. Holmes," he answered. "Unfortunately, a number of our records were lost in a small fire several years ago."

"Holmes, obviously something about this shield has struck a chord with you. Would you care to enlighten the rest of us?"

Holmes smiled and said, "My apologies. However, unless, I am very much mistaken, I believe we are looking at a shield that quite possibly belonged to Jacques de Molay, for that certainly appears to be his coat of arms."

Although the name sounded vaguely familiar, I couldn't pin it down.

Fortunately, neither could Rotondo who admitted, "I'm afraid I don't know who that is."

"Jacques de Molay was a French Crusader. He and many other French crusaders were arrested and imprisoned in 1307. After several years during which he was tortured and confessed to various crimes, only to subsequently recant his admissions when the torture ceased, de Molay and two of his followers were burned at the stake in 1314. As you might expect, many historians now believe the charges, which included blasphemy and heresy, were manufactured by the King of France.

"However, the most important detail – certainly more significant than any of that – is the fact that Jacques de Molay was the last Grand Master of the Knights Templar."

Chapter 2

"The Knights Templar? You can't be serious, Holmes!" I exclaimed. "Why would anyone today be concerned about the actions of a group of Crusaders more than half a millennium ago?"

"An excellent question, Watson. Although I must admit that I can think of a great many reasons," said Holmes. "There are vestiges of the Templars throughout England. In fact, right here in London, we have a rather stunning example."

"I assume you are referring to the Temple Church, Mr. Holmes," interjected Rotondo.

"Indeed, I am," replied my friend.

"But that's a legal college," I exclaimed.

"Yes, but it wasn't always so," replied Holmes. "Built in the mid-12th century, the Round Church, as it is sometimes known, was constructed to serve as London's Jerusalem. In fact, the Magna Carta was negotiated in that very Temple, In short, the Temple was the birthplace of British common law, which in turn was transported to the Colonies. But enough of that, let me examine the coin.

"In fact," he continued, "you may have heard the theory put forth that anyplace in England with Temple in its name can be traced back to the Templars."

"I have certainly heard that," added Rotondo as he reached into the cabinet, picked up the coin and handed it to Holmes. After walking to a window for better light, Holmes withdrew his lens from his coat pocket and began to study the coin in earnest. Knowing the discussion would resume only when Holmes was ready, I busied myself studying the swords and daggers in one of the display cases.

I was so deep in thought, I failed to hear Rotondo creep up behind me. "Those are some nasty bits of work aren't they?" he asked, pointing to the case. Then, gesturing towards Holmes, he asked, "Is he always like this?"

"When he is on a case, he is quite often the picture of intense concentration."

"So then this *is* a case," the curator remarked with a slight quiver of excitement in his voice.

At that moment, Holmes turned to us, "A case, I should think so. Intriguing, most certainly! And Watson will tell you there is nothing so interesting as that which seems commonplace on the surface, but poses far more questions when you begin to examine its roots."

"What about the coin, Holmes?"

"Indeed," he said, holding up what appeared to be a bright silver penny. "I have no doubt this coin was once carried by a Crusader. It is known as a silver billon – not to be confused with bullion – Denier of Antioch. Relatively rare, these hand-hammered coins date from the mid-12th to the mid-13th century."

As he handed it to me, he continued, "Notice the flared-end cross *pattee* and Crusader's crescent on one side while the other side displays a Crusading King adorned in chainmail with a cross on his medieval helmet. Right here," he said, indicating two small scratch marks, "is where it was attached to a watch chain by a bezel. Presumably its shape, far from a perfect circle, allowed to be jarred loose from its holder."

"So now we have a Crusader coin found next to the shield of a Templar Grand Master?" I asked.

"It would appear so, Watson."

"Where is this going, Holmes?"

"Right now, I haven't a clue, but I will attempt to follow the trail if I am able."

Turning to Rotondo, Holmes said, "Would you mind if I examined the shield? Also," he added, holding up the coin, "I should like to hold on to this for a bit? I have a few experts I should like to have examine it."

"By all means, Mr. Holmes. Return it at your leisure."

After pocketing the coin, Holmes removed the small shield and brought it to a display case by the same window where the light was better. He then began to examine the front of the shield quite carefully. After several minutes, he sighed and then turned the shield over.

I watched as he examined the strap that would secure the shield to the arm and the handle where the knight would grasp it. Suddenly, he broke the silence as he said, "How very odd."

Rotondo and I looked at each other, but we both realized he was speaking to himself rather than us. We watched in silence as he continued his examination. He then took out a small notebook of his own and jotted something down.

After he had finished his inspection, he turned to the curator and said. "I have a question and a suggestion. First, since you have the shield, do you know if you have the sword of de Molay?"

"I couldn't say for certain, Mr. Holmes. As I mentioned, armour and weapons are rather outside my area of expertise."

"Do you mind if I take a quick look?"

"Not at all, Mr. Holmes. But before you do, may I ask what your suggestion is?"

"You might consider changing the locks on the cases to something a bit more secure."

"I shall do it today. Is there anything else?"

"For the next week or two, you may want to station a guard or guards in this room. When your visitor discovers his loss, he may well return here to look for it."

"Thank you, Mr. Holmes. I shall make those arrangements as well."

Holmes then spent the next two hours, far from the "quick look" he had promised, examining every blade in the room, and given his mood when he finished, I could see that he was irritated.

We then bade Rotondo farewell. When we exited the Collection, it was a glorious spring day, so Holmes suggested we savour the weather and return home on foot.

After a few minutes, I asked, "What was all that about with the swords?"

"On the inside of the shield was etched the motto of the Templars: *Non nobis, Domine, non nobis, sed nomini tuo da gloria,* which translates to: Not to us, Lord, not to us, but to your name give the glory."

"Is that significant?"

"I think the message contains a code."

"Why do you say that?"

"Some of the letters appear to have been etched more deeply than others."

"And what does it tell you?"

"I'm afraid that will require some research and at least two pipes, possibly three."

As we turned onto Baker Street, I asked, "Do you really think the intruder will return to Hertford House?"

"If the coin is dear to him, and I suspect it is, I am certain he will return to look for it there."

"And when he is captured?"

"I should like to ascertain his interest in the Templars. Exactly how much do you know about those fabled fighters?" asked Holmes.

"Not as much as I would like, and quite obviously, not nearly as much as you."

Holmes laughed and then proceeded to outline a very concise history of the the Poor Fellow-Soldiers of Christ and of the Temple of Solomon, also known as the Order of Solomon's Temple, the Knights Templar, or simply the Templars.

What follows is a greatly condensed version of Holmes's retelling. There have been many volumes devoted to the origins and history of the Templars, and it soon became apparent that Holmes was familiar with a great many of them.

"The group was founded at the beginning of the 12th century, perhaps two decades after the end of the First Crusade. If you believe the legend, it began with a mere nine knights who dedicated themselves to providing safe conduct for Christian pilgrims who wished to visit sites in the Holy Land, especially in Jerusalem. Although the Holy City was held by Christians after the First Crusade, there were brigands along much of the route ready to pounce upon the unguarded pilgrim.

"Men who joined the Templars were required to take vows of poverty, chastity and obedience. They were, in truth, warrior monks. They quickly gained the favour and protection of Pope Innocent II and found themselves the beneficiaries of generous gifts of land and wealth – donated by monarchs and nobles throughout Europe – in order to sustain the order."

"But what about their vow of poverty?"

Holmes continued as if he had not heard me, "In the Second Crusade, the Templars were instrumental in routing the great Saladin's army at the Battle of Montgisard. With the support of several successive popes as well as a number of prominent churchmen, including St. Bernard of Clairveaux, the Templars were lauded as warriors. At the same time, they also established a revolutionary system of banking. Pilgrims embarking for the Holy Land could deposit money with the Templars in various European countries, receive a letter of credit and then reclaim their funds once they reached Jerusalem.

"They also received considerable donations from many monarchs, including King Henry II, which allowed the Templars to establish financial networks across the whole of Christendom. They were the precursor to the Dutch East India Company, if you will."

"Yes, yes, this is all very interesting, I'm sure," I interrupted, "but what do the exploits and business dealings of a group of knights founded in the Holy Land nearly 800 years ago have to do with anything in England today?"

"The specifics remain as yet unknown, but while the French adhere to *cherchez la femme*, I am far more inclined to consider the Latin phrase: *Cui bono*?

"Just within England, as I said, the Templars were gifted large tracts of land; as a result of which, they often purchased and managed farms and vineyards. In addition to their agrarian endeavours, they constructed stone cathedrals and castles – a number of which are still standing today.

"Truth be told, there was little that escaped the touch of the Templars. They were involved in manufacturing as well as importing and exporting. To facilitate the latter, they had their own fleet of ships; and at one point they even owned the entire island of Cyprus, which they had purchased from Richard the Lionheart. If there was money to be made, the Templars were involved."

"What happened to the knights and the vast fortune they had accrued?"

"In short, the knights were betrayed. King Philip the Fair of France, always in need of funds, set his sights on the Templars' treasure. After forcing the College of Cardinals to elect his man – Clement V – as pope, Philip had the papacy moved from Rome to Avignon – a move sometimes referred to as the 'Babylonian captivity of the Papacy.'

"Working with a succession of popes, each one weaker than his predecessor, Philip orchestrated the arrest and imprisonment of most of the Templars. On Friday the 13th of October, 1307 – yes, much of the superstition about the date appears to have had its origins with the Templars – Philip implemented a secret plan that had been months in the making. Hundreds of Templars were arrested and imprisoned and much of their treasure confiscated. Accused of an array of crimes, the Templars were tortured until they 'confessed.'

"However, when they were brought before the pope, they recanted their confessions. This back-and-forth wrangling went on for seven years until on the morning of 11th of March – though there is some disagreement about the date – de Molay and two other leading Templars were burned at the stake on the Ile des Javiaux in the Seine."

"My word, Holmes, what an extraordinary tale."

"It has an even more bizarre conclusion, old friend. If legend is to be believed, just as he was about to be burned, de Molay cursed the pope and King Philip, telling them they would have to answer to God for their sins. The pope died about five weeks later and Philip within a year."

"And now it appears we have someone with connections to the Templars breaking into a museum but stealing nothing. It boggles the imagination."

"Truly. Unfortunately, we don't have much to go on – just a small coin and some tallow drippings."

"I've seen you start with far less than that," I offered.

"True, I was hopeful of a challenge, and now I have one. In the future, Watson, remind me to be more circumspect about those things for which I wish."

By this time, we had reached our lodgings, and as we entered, Mrs. Hudson emerged from her parlour, "Thank goodness you are home, gentlemen."

"What is wrong, dear lady?"

"There's nothing wrong with me, Doctor, but I'm not certain I can say the same for the young woman in my sitting room. She's been waiting some time to see Mr. Holmes."

"What on Earth?" Holmes exclaimed.

"She arrived more than an hour ago, and she appeared quite distressed. I know how particular you are about strangers in your rooms, Mr. Holmes, so I invited her to remain with me until you returned."

"That was most kind of you," I said shooting Holmes a glance. "If you would be so kind as to take us to her, we will hear what she has to say."

Chapter 3

We followed our landlady down the hall into her sitting room, where a young woman, perhaps 25 years of age, sat sipping a cup of tea. Modestly dressed, she was slender with raven hair and a dark complexion. She also had stunning blue eyes. She was what I believe many refer to as "dark Irish."

"My dear," said Mrs. Hudson, "these are the gentlemen you've been waiting for. This is Mr. Holmes and that is Dr. Watson."

She smiled at both of us and said, "Thank you for seeing me, gentlemen. I do hope that I have not disrupted your day to an irreparable degree, but I have nowhere else to turn."

"Let us begin at the beginning," said Holmes. "You are?"

"I am so sorry. I appear to have forgot my manners that's how distressing this whole situation has become." She paused and then said, "My name is Caroline Green, and I must confess I am at my wits' end."

"Pray tell, what seems to be the cause of your distress?" I asked.

"I traveled here from Royston this morning because of my father. Lately he has been acting quite peculiar, and

I am worried he may do something foolish – something that might cause irrevocable harm both to himself and our family's good name."

"Your father wouldn't be Sir Richard Green, *aide de camp* to General Sir Charles Warren, by any chance?" asked Holmes.

"Mr. Holmes, you astonish me. My father has been with Sir Charles since the early 1860s. His first assignment was to assist the general and Major-General Frome with the mapping of Gibraltar."

Holmes then suggested we move to our sitting room, and he asked Mrs. Hudson if she would be so kind as to prepare another pot of tea.

After we had moved upstairs, Holmes picked up the conversation exactly where it had ended. "I assume then that your father was also with Warren in 1867 when he conducted his survey of Palestine and undertook one of the first major excavations of the Temple Mount in Jerusalem?"

"Indeed, it was because of that work that Sir Charles was promoted to captain and my father to lieutenant."

"Didn't Warren also discover a series of tunnels underneath the Temple Mount?"

"That is also true. In fact he has written a number of books about his time there."

"Yes, yes, I am familiar with his scholarly endeavours and I have copies of his *Survey of Western Palestine-Jerusalem* as well as *The Recovery of Jerusalem, Underground Jerusalem* and *The Land of Promise* on my shelves," Holmes said gesturing vaguely towards the bookcases that were groaning under the weight of his yearbooks and various other tomes.

"My father played a major role in all of Sir Charles's discoveries and he contributed to all of the books as well. However, he received virtually no credit although the general did acknowledge him in the books. While being given such short shrift didn't seem to bother my father, I must admit that the rest of the family was rather put out."

"I have heard rumours to the effect that Warren can be rather chary with sharing the credit," said Holmes.

As I listened to this, I must admit I was more than a bit taken aback. Although I knew Holmes to be well-versed in an array of diverse subjects, I must admit that I was stunned to find he had at some point turned his attention to archaeology and the excavation of Jerusalem.

"I am still puzzled, Miss Green. Your father appears to have led an exemplary life so what has he done that has brought you to my door? And pray be precise with regard to details."

"There were points about which General Warren and my father disagreed – sometime vehemently."

Holmes said nothing for several seconds, lost as he was in concentration. Finally, he broke his silence, saying, "Please continue."

"Over the past few years, my father has become quite irritable, snapping at the servants, yelling at my mother and me. His whole personality and demeanour changed. He would often spend nights at his club in London – something he had never done previously. Then finally, three days ago, he left the house in the morning, and he has not returned since."

"Miss Green, have you ever heard of the Knights Templar?" asked Holmes.

"My uncle is a barrister, Mr. Holmes. He has told me stories about the Middle and Inner Temples here in London and their origins. However, I must admit that beyond that, I really don't know that much about them."

"The uncle – mother's brother or father's?" asked Holmes.

"My mother's," she replied.

"Did he and your father get on?"

"With father being away from home so much, I really couldn't say."

"Would you know if your father happened to be familiar with the Templars?"

"I cannot say for certain, but given what little I know of them and my uncle, I find it highly unlikely that he would not know something of them."

"I rather suspected as much. Has your father made any new acquaintances of late?"

"Although father was never a very sociable man to begin with, I have heard from the servants that he has been visited several times by two men over the last few months. Sometimes they come together; on other occasions one or the other has come alone."

"Have you ever seen or met either of these men?"

"I saw one of them once from a distance. His carriage was just leaving our estate as I arrived home."

"Could you identify this man?"

"I'm afraid not. I only caught a quick glimpse of a profile as his carriage passed mine."

"Perhaps when you return home, you might make a few discreet inquiries of the servants."

"I shall do that," she replied, "and I will post an answer either tonight or first thing tomorrow morning."

"Do you have any brothers or sisters?"

"No Mister Holmes. I am an only child, and my mother passed away a year ago."

"Very well, Miss Green. Now let us get to the matter at hand, shall we? You have hinted at some aberrant behavior on your father's part of late, but unless you tell me exactly what he has done that has brought you to my door, I am afraid that I cannot provide the help you seek."

Our guest appeared a bit flustered by Holmes' directness; finally, after a rather awkward silence she said, "Mr. Holmes, I think my father is being forced to aid in some sort of archaeological expedition."

"You should have said that at the beginning," Holmes stated. "Why do you say it now?"

"My father was never jealous of General Warren, but I think he believes he never received proper recognition for his contributions. I think the men that came to our house offered my father a chance at the glory he felt was rightfully his, and he has taken it."

"I believe General Warren has been back and forth to Sinai and the Sudan several times in recent years," I offered.

"Yes, I know for certain the Admiralty sent Sir Charles to Sinai to ascertain the fate of the archaeological expedition led by Professor Edward Palmer," said Holmes.

"If memory serves, Warren discovered the expedition members had been robbed and murdered, located their remains, and then brought their killers to justice."

"What you say is true, Mr. Holmes. For his exploits, Sir Charles was created a Knight Commander of the Order of St. Michael in 1883 and he was also awarded an Order of the Medjidie, Third Class by the Egyptian government. That same year, he was made a Knight of Justice of the Order of St. John of Jerusalem and then last year he was elected a Fellow of the Royal Society.

"And do you know who was at his side each and every time and whose only recognition was a mention in a book read by ..." I'm not certain what her next words might have been, but it struck me that she suddenly recalled that Holmes possessed all of Warren's books.

I saw Holmes smile in spite of himself as he realized the import of her unspoken words.

"Men have done far worse for far less," Holmes stated. "I will make some inquiries and let you know as soon as I have something of substance to report."

She left us her information and then departed.

No sooner had I heard the door close then Holmes said, "What do you make of that, Watson?"

"She seemed a charming enough young lady, and I am certain that her concern for her father is genuine."

"That isn't what I meant at all. Consider, first we are summoned to the Wallace Collection where a Templar coin has been left and someone appears to have shown an express interest in the shield of Jacques de Molay, the last Grand Master of that order.

"Then we return home to find a woman waiting for us, who claims her father has been acting irrationally of late – and that same father has spent much of his adult life in the area where the Templars were founded and where they conducted many of their early campaigns."

"I would say that is either an incredible coincidence or something nefarious is being plotted – something into which you have been drawn."

After lighting a cigarette, Holmes looked at me and said, "You know I do not believe in coincidence; therefore, I am inclined to the latter possibility with a few minor modifications."

"Such as?"

"I must confess that my notions in that regard are but vague at the present. The only thing I can say for certain is that I feel a trip to Royston is order."

"Royston, the home town of Captain Green? Why? What is in Royston that warrants a visit?"

"Have you never heard of the Royston Cave?"

"Can't say that I have."

"The cave, if we may call it such, was discovered in the middle of the last century, 1742 if I recall correctly, by workmen who were digging a hole and discovered a buried millstone. After it was excavated, they found a passage leading to a subterranean chamber. They lowered a young boy in by a rope who reported the existence of the underground room.

"Once the passage had been properly cleared and reinforced, they discovered it led to a circular, bell-shaped room which had been cut into the chalk bedrock. It is more than 20 feet high and some 17 feet in diameter.

"To the best of my knowledge, the cave is unique in Britain for its numerous medieval carvings on the walls – most of which, as you might expect, are religious in nature although there are a few exceptions.

"But one of the carvings, although partially eroded depicts two figures close together, perhaps riding a horse."

"Perhaps?"

"The carving has been damaged, so the horse remains a mere supposition."

"I still don't see what that has to do…"

"That same image of two men sharing a horse is a symbol closely associated with ..." and here Holmes paused to light another cigarette – and I am sure to build a bit of dramatic tension of which he is so fond, before finishing with the words, "the Knights Templar." With that he headed towards his bedroom, presumably to pack a few things and change his clothes.

"So we are going to visit Royston to see a cave that may or may not be connected to the Templars."

Turning back at the doorway, he said, "Because it is a cave which I believe to be linked to the Knights Templar, albeit in a rather tenuous fashion. Still, I won't know more until I have actually examined it." With that he began to consult his Bradshaw. "There's a train leaving King's Cross in an hour. Can you be ready?"

"Certainly, but why exactly are we going?"

"Because it's patently obvious that someone wants us in Royston or, at the very least, out of London."

Turning back once again, he rang the bell for the page, "Before we do anything else, I must send a couple of telegrams."

As he was writing out the messages, he mused more to himself more than me, "I wonder why Miss Green never mentioned it. How every odd."

Chapter 4

When we descended the stairs perhaps forty minutes later, Holmes said "I have one more bit of business to which I must attend – it shouldn't take long." Walking outside he soon spotted one of his Irregulars and within a few minutes, the boy had scampered off and returned with Wiggins, the unofficial leader of Holmes's contingent of street Arabs.

After a few minutes of earnest conversation, which I was unable to overhear, Holmes gave the boy some coins and he snatched them with a grin and then scampered down the street in the direction of Regent's Park. After Holmes had joined me in the cab, I was tempted to ask what the business with Wiggins was about, but I refrained.

Although the station was bustling, we managed to secure a first-class cabin on the 2:30 train to Royston. The journey is a relatively short one, perhaps 60 miles, and Holmes, surprisingly, was in quite a jovial mood. He nattered on about an array of topics and really warmed to his subject when he began discussing the origin of the name Royston.

"At some point in the misty past, a cross was erected by the town's crossroads. Throughout the centuries it has been known by several different names including Royse's, Rohesia's, and Roisia's Cross," he said, spelling each of the variations out. "As a result the settlement was first called Crux Roesia or Roisia's Cross, but by the 14th century – note the date, old man – it had become simply Roisia's Town which eventually gave way to Roiston or Royston."

"Fascinating," I lied, trying hard to conceal my disinterest. When I glanced at Holmes, I believe that he was aware of my mendacity but had decided to let it go. Instead, he turned to the subject of the cave.

"I believe the year was 1742 when the cave was discovered. It actually lies beneath a street named Ickneid Way. After the find, one of the enterprising townsmen, a man named Thomas Watson – no relation, I trust – had a shaft dug from his house into the cave and virtually took possession of it. In fact, anyone who wished to see the cave had to pay an admission fee. Quite the enterprising fellow when you consider he had no legal claim to the land whatsoever.

"Then in 1852, Joseph Beldam, a Royston-born barrister, as well as an historian and author, began a serious investigation of the cave. Working with him was a man named Edmund Nunn, who also happened to serve as the curator of Royston Museum. Their findings were published in a report which was presented to The Royal

Society of Antiquaries. The report also included drawings they had made of some of the carvings."

Holmes continued on with his explanation of all things related to the Royston Cave, but I was more focused on why someone would wish us to leave London. The next thing I knew the conductor was calling "Royston," and a few minutes later Holmes and I were in a dog cart heading for the entrance to the cave.

We stopped in front of a shoe shop with a sign proclaiming "Boots Repaired" in the window. A short man with a cherubic face and glistening pate came out from the shop to meet us. "Would you be Mr. Sherlock Holmes?" he inquired.

"I am," replied my friend, "and this is my friend and colleague Dr. John Watson."

"Ah, sir, I received your telegram and you are welcome here." he said. Then turning to me, he positively beamed as he continued, "Dr. Watson, such a pleasure to meet you. I do enjoy your stories in *The Strand*. I look forward to them each month. But I'm forgetting my manners." Extending his hand, he said, "I am George Pool, and I own the house that contains the entrance to the cave."

"Mr. Pool, I regret that my time is limited…," said Holmes.

Before he could finish, Pool replied, "Follow me." He led us into a narrow alley next to the shoe repair shop and after about thirty feet, we turned into a passageway that was even more narrow than the alley. Pool handed each of us a dark lantern and then said, "I have taken the liberty of lighting a number of torches in the cave so that you may be able to examine the carvings quite closely if you desire."

Holmes thanked him and then after a short descent, we found ourselves in a bell-like structure that had been hewn from the soft chalk rock. The walls were covered with carvings of all shapes and sizes. Holmes slipped Pool a few notes, thanked him and told him he would notify him when he had completed his examination.

After Pool had left, I said to Holmes, "What is it exactly that you hope to discover down here?"

"If I knew the answer to that, I could have saved us a trip, but all my instincts tell me there is something here – a clue of some sort, perhaps – waiting to be discovered. See if any of the carvings strike a chord with you."

With that, Holmes began to examine each carving as closely as possible. I heard him muttering to himself, "St. Catherine … Richard the Lionheart … St. George … The Crucifixion … Interesting, quite interesting. I wonder …"

"What's that, Holmes?" I asked as I made my way to him.

"You see this figure here? He appears to be bound to a stake and he's wearing what appears to be heretic's cap."

"Heretic's cap?"

"Yes, heretics were often forced to wear a conical hat, similar to a bishop's mitre, as they were led to their execution. It was nothing more than another form of mockery. Given the cap, the bindings, the stake – if indeed it is that – I wonder if that might not be a depiction of Jacques de Molay."

"I would imagine it is. After all, you said the cave is linked to the Templars."

"If I recall, my exact words were 'the cave is *believed* to be linked to the Templars.' There are just as many scholars who dispute that notion, so one must tread carefully with such assertions."

"Well, I found a crude depiction of two men who may be sharing a horse over here, and I am certain you said that was an image associated with the Templars – emphasizing their vow of poverty, I believe."

"Touché, Watson. Hoisted by my own petard."

After he had spent at least two hours inspecting the carvings, during which time we were visited by Pool on no less than three different occasions, Holmes seemed to give up. "There may be a clue here," he sighed, "but dashed if I can find it."

As we were about to leave, I pointed to what appeared to be a hole high up in the wall. "What do you suppose that was for?"

Looking up to a rather large opening perhaps ten feet off the ground, Holmes added, "I believe that was the original entrance. From it, the knights could have stepped directly onto a platform and then they would descend down here by means of a ladder.

"If you look down, you will see that there are holes in the floor. Many scholars think there may have been a platform in here at one time and that the platform and the niches above it may have been used for storage at some point."

With that Holmes returned his gaze to the floor and then back up to the holes. "I wonder..." he said, letting the words trail off. He stepped over and stood below the opening in question.

"What are you thinking, Holmes?"

"If the niches above were once used for storage, I wonder if the vacant hole might not be used for concealment. Come here, Watson, and put your hands together so that I can take a look in that recess."

With just my hands as a step, Holmes was still a few inches too short, so undignified as it may have been, I allowed him to stand on my shoulders. Although he is lean, I should not like to have had to bear Holmes up there for any length of time.

Although I was facing the wall and could see nothing, my heart raced when I heard him exclaim, "Halloa! What have we here?"

Jumping down, he held out a small silver coin that appeared similar to that which had been found in the gallery. He also held a small piece of dried and weathered paper.

"Something was concealed there. The dust has been disturbed, and quite recently I should think. This is a piece of vellum, so there was a document, or documents, stored there. This coin was all the way in the back which I only discovered because I was looking for it."

"You were? Why on Earth did you expect to find a coin in such a place?"

"Because I think we are being manipulated, Watson. And I must admit I have mixed emotions about admitting it." After making that pronouncement, he said no more on the subject, despite my imprecations.

We continued to examine the carvings for a few more minutes and then Holmes looked at his watch and said, "I think I have done all I can here, we should probably be going."

When we ascended to the street level, I was surprised to discover the door had been closed behind us. I pushed to open it, but it wouldn't budge. For a brief second, the thought crossed my mind we had been locked into the cave deliberately. I thought that one of Holmes's many enemies might have finally caught up with him.

However, before I could say anything, Pool opened the door himself. "It's three o'clock, Mr. Holmes, I was just coming down to fetch you and the doctor."

"We finished a few minutes early. I want to thank you again for locking the door and allowing us to examine the cave with a degree of privacy. However, I do have one question: Has anyone brought a ladder into the cave recently?"

"A ladder? Not as I can recall," Pool responded.

"Any groups of men, then?"

"It's certainly possible. When I'm not here either my wife or my oldest son handles the visitors. I can check with them if you like."

"That won't be necessary," said Holmes as though it were a matter of no concern.

By this time we had followed Pool into his shop. Holmes once again thanked him for his courtesy and Pool then asked us if we would sign the guest book. As we did so, he informed us, "A number of important people have visited the cave over the years. Why back at the beginning of the century, long before my time, I'm told King Louis XVIII of France went down into the cave. He was living in England in exile at the time."

"Oh," I responded, "you don't say." I was certain that Pool was exaggerating and telling stories that couldn't possibly be checked. However, when I looked at Holmes, I could see that Pool's story had touched him in some way.

For the next hour, Holmes was a study in silence. There was no conversation during our cab ride to the station, and the quiet continued during the forty minutes we spent waiting for the train. Having seen my friend in this type of mood before, I knew it was better to hold my tongue. He would speak when he was ready and neither heaven nor earth could move him until that time.

Finally, after we were on our way back to London, he suddenly said, "So, Watson, what did you think of Pool's story about the royal visitor to Royston?"

"Sounds like a bit of stuff and nonsense to me. Something to tell visitors to make the cave more of an attraction."

"That may be some truth in that assertion, but still, Pool was telling the truth. However, the most important fact is that Louis XVIII was a member of the House of Bourbon, a family that can trace its origins back to 13th-century France and perhaps even further. The history of the Bourbons is a convoluted one, but there is a branch of the family that boasts of an uninterrupted line all the way back to Capetian kings – of whom Philip IV was one. I trust you begin to see the connection."

"You said Philip was the king who had the Templars arrested and their leaders executed?"

"Indeed, and while doing so, relieved them of much of the wealth and property they had accumulated – despite their vow of poverty. As you might expect, monarchs in a number of other countries soon followed suit. Although some actually handed over the wealth to the Knights Hospitaller, others proved a bit more rapacious.

"There's another connection between a distant relative of Louis and the Templars but that's going to require a great deal more research before I can comment further.

"Still, I must admit that certain connections, although unexpected, are becoming obvious. They are tenuous at best, but they can't all be coincidences. These are deep waters, Watson, and no doubt they will get deeper and darker still.

"By the way, I trust you noticed in the guest book that a group of three men visited the cave last week – one of whom was named Philip Bourbon." Having said that, he lapsed back into silence and remained that way for the duration of our trip – and the day.

Chapter 5

The next morning, Holmes had risen long before I and departed our flat, so I ate a solitary breakfast and perused the morning papers. I saw nothing there that I thought would appeal to my friend's love of the unusual.

After a long day at my practice, I returned home to find that Holmes was once again nowhere to be found. When I asked, Mrs. Hudson informed me that he had returned early in the afternoon, eaten a sandwich with coffee and then ventured back out in what she called "another one of his dress-up outfits." According to her, Holmes had departed wearing some sort of dark robe with a hood and sandals. As you might expect, I found the whole notion rather fanciful and more than a bit surprising. Still, I had known my friend to do stranger things.

His absence continued for two more days and then finally on the fourth day, he returned home in time for supper, dressed in a black, hooded robe and wearing a knotted rope as a belt. "Holmes, you never fail to amaze me, but I think you have outdone yourself this time."

Laughing, he said, "Allow me to change, and I will explain everything." A few minutes later he emerged from his bedroom looking much like his old self.

"I can only gather you've been digging into the records regarding the Knights Templar."

"There's been a bit of that. I've also made inquiries about Captain Green; unfortunately, I have nothing new to report on that front. Still, it has been a rather productive few days. I have visited several monasteries – including one in Bristol, one in Cambridgeshire and two in Essex – all of which were controlled by the Knights Templar at one time."

"I had no idea they had so many outposts in England."

At that Holmes laughed, "There are more than thirty former Templar monasteries and churches in England – and that's not including those located in Scotland and Ireland."

"And did you learn anything that might help us in this case?"

"A snippet here, a fragment there, it falls to me to assemble the pieces of this giant mosaic into an intelligible whole, and while my progress may be slow, it nevertheless continues apace."

"Speaking of progress, were you able to learn anything from the coin found at the Wallace Collection?"

"Sadly, no. I sent it, as well as the one we found in Royston, to a numismatist friend at the British Museum. He confirmed they were both silver billon Deniers; unfortunately, while they are not common, they are not as rare as I had believed, so ends that thread."

We enjoyed a leisurely dinner, and I then went to my club leaving Holmes to his own devices.

The next morning at perhaps eight o'clock, as we were eating breakfast and perusing the papers, I heard the bell ring. "Could this be a client calling so early?" I asked.

"You know my hours are anything but regular," replied Holmes, "and as you might imagine my clients' hours are equally varied."

A minute later there was a knock on the door. "Come in, Mrs. Hudson," said Holmes.

Our landlady entered and said, "There is a gentleman hoping that you might see him, Mr. Holmes. He sent up his card."

Holmes took the card, looked at it and I saw a look of astonishment flash across his features. Handing me the card, he said, "What do you make of this, Watson?" Taking it, I looked at the stiff piece of cardboard and was surprised to see the name:

Capt. Richard Green, Ret.
British Royal Engineers
The Hamlet, Royston

"Well this is certainly a surprise," I said.

"Do show the gentleman up, please, Mrs. Hudson."

A moment later, a rather tall, thin man entered the room. He looked to be in his mid-50s and his darkened, leathery skin had the appearance of someone who had spent long hours outside in sunnier climes. He had a head of thinning blond hair and intelligent brown eyes. I remember thinking, his daughter must have got her looks from her mother.

"Mr. Holmes, it is a pleasure to meet you," said our guest, and turning to me he said, "and you must be Dr. Watson."

"What brings you to Baker Street, Capt. Green?"

"It's just Mister Green now. I separated from the army several years ago."

"Still, how may I be of service?" continued Holmes undeterred.

"Actually, I am wondering how I might be of service to you, Mr. Holmes. I have heard from several quarters that you have been making inquiries about me. I would have been here sooner had I known, but I have just returned the day before yesterday from an extended stay in France."

"France? Your excursion to the Continent wouldn't have anything to do with the Knights Templar?" Holmes asked in an unusual display of directness.

The look on our guest's face was one of both shock and bewilderment. For a second he seemed as though he were trying to recover from having been poleaxed. After regaining his composure, he said, "I have heard of your powers of deduction, Mr. Holmes, but that is truly amazing. How could you possibly know of my current research? I have taken great pains to keep it under wraps."

Holmes smiled that enigmatic smile and simply said, "I am Sherlock Holmes. It is my business to know things."

"Well, then I must ask you to keep my secret. There is a great deal riding on my research and inquiries. If I am correct in my assumptions, it may cause people to look at history in an entirely different way. Actually, were it not for some personal business which required my presence here, I would still be in France."

"How long had you planned to stay abroad?"

"As long as it takes. I have been in France for nearly six weeks and was prepared to remain there six months if necessary."

"So you are searching for Templar records in France that you are hoping will exonerate Jacques de Molay and the other Templars accused of heresy." Holmes' words were a statement rather than a question, and again our guest had to pause and gather himself before answering.

"I have heard of your abilities, Mr. Holmes, and now that I have witnessed them first-hand, I must say the rumours do not do you justice."

Always susceptible to flattery, Holmes allowed himself a slight smile. "So I have hit the mark?"

"In a manner of speaking. At any rate, you are very close. However, I am pursuing two lines of inquiry – quite separate and distinct yet related. I hope you will understand if I choose not to elaborate on my efforts at the present."

Joining the conversation, I offered, "If anyone should appreciate a degree of reticence, it would be Holmes. I daresay the man prides himself on his laconicism."

"At any rate," continued Green, "my suspicions are simply that at this time. They have yet to be confirmed, but that is something on which I am labouring assiduously."

I thought to myself, Green and Holmes are indeed birds of a feather.

"Do you believe the proof still exists – all these centuries later – that will allow you to confirm your thesis?" asked Holmes.

"I cannot say for certain. I hope I may be able to locate enough documents, both here in England and abroad, to support my contentions under the most withering scrutiny. As I indicated, there is also a secondary reason motivating my search but we need not discuss that at present."

"As you wish, but I assure you I work best with a full knowledge of my client's motives and activities. Now, have you ever been to the Wallace Collection here in London?"

"Many times," replied Green. "I know they have a shield that belonged to Jacques de Molay, and I believe they have several other Templar weapons – although I am not certain they realize what they have."

Holmes smiled and his next question took both of us by surprise, "Have you ever broken into the Wallace Collection?"

I was once again stunned at my friend's bluntness while our guest seemed taken aback for a third time. "I have no need to break into the collection, Mr. Holmes. The curator, Paul Rotondo, is an old friend of mine and has allowed me, when necessary, to conduct my research there in his office – undisturbed."

"Now, if you don't mind," Green said, "I think it's my turn to ask a few questions. Why did you ask about the Wallace Collection?"

"They have had a nocturnal visitor on several occasions in recent months and whoever it may be appears to be as interested in the Templars as you are."

"I was afraid of that," said Green, and before either of us could ask why, he followed up with, "You have been looking for me, Mr. Holmes. May I ask why?"

"Your daughter, Caroline, came to us several days ago. She has been most worried about you and sought my help in trying to locate you."

"That's quite remarkable, Mr. Holmes. Unfortunately, it's not true."

"I sat here and spoke with her," I said. "She is quite a charming young woman."

"I know neither who contacted you nor with whom you spoke. However, I can say with absolute certainty that it was not my daughter, Caroline. You see she passed away nine months ago. She was killed in a riding accident when she was thrown from her horse."

Chapter 6

As you might expect, there was a prolonged and awkward silence in the room following Green's somber pronouncement. Holmes and I looked at each other, and I could see he was as baffled as I. Suddenly, he sprang into action. Jumping from his chair, he ran to the window where he surreptitiously studied the ebb and flow of the people on Baker Street below him.

Without turning from the window, Holmes asked, "How did you learn that I was looking for you? Who was it exactly that told you and when?"

"I can't see that it's of any importance…"

Before he could say another word, Holmes cut him off. Although he was not angry, he was certainly forceful when he stated, "Capt. Green, you are an expert in your field. I would not even begin to think of questioning your methods nor telling you how to conduct your research as you delve into the mysteries of the past. I beg that you will extend me the same courtesy as I try to solve the puzzles of the present."

Suitably chastised, Green said, "A researcher at the British Museum named Nancy Barbuto."

"Indeed," replied Holmes. "I should have known. Like myself, Miss Barbuto has a large network of contacts.

She is a superb organizer. Anyone working in her area had better leave it as pristine as they found it or they may well suffer her wrath."

"I don't know who told her," Green said, "but she has helped me on any number of occasions in the past and when she speaks it is with a certain clarity that is seldom found today."

Holmes turned to face us with a slight smile on his face and without knowing anymore, I could tell that he and this woman were in some way kindred spirits.

"At any rate, she seemed overjoyed to see me yesterday afternoon, and she quickly pulled me aside. She asked me if I had heard of you. When I admitted that I was but vaguely acquainted with your name, she told me a bit about you and said that you were looking for me. She said, 'If Mr. Holmes is looking for you, it must be something important.' Then she gave me your address and suggested I call on you as soon as I could."

"Do you think anyone may have followed you here?" asked Holmes.

"I really don't know. I certainly wasn't looking for anyone."

Turning to me, Holmes said, "Watson, I'd like you to fill our guest in on everything that has happened thus far." Turning to Green, he said, "You see, I am willing to be totally forthcoming – even if you are not."

As Holmes headed towards his bedroom, I asked, "And what will you be doing?"

"Taking a closer look at the denizens of Baker Street in the hopes of seeing an unfamiliar face or two."

Perhaps a quarter of an hour later, Holmes emerged from his bedroom and the transformation was remarkable. In place of the debonair detective, there now stood a fully bewhiskered constable, complete with truncheon and the tall helmet favoured by those who worked in the poorer sections of London. The coat was obviously padded, for Holmes's girth had increased considerably, but unless I had seen the transformation myself, I'm not certain I would have recognized my friend had I passed him on the street.

It was obvious Green was stunned at the change, but he said nothing. "What would you like us to do, Holmes?" I asked.

"Give me fifteen minutes to ascertain whether Captain Green has been followed. Then use the back entrance and escort him to the Northumberland. When you arrive, book a room under the name Jefferson Hope. I shall join you in a few hours. Until we know a great deal more about why people are so eager to locate you and apparently even more desperate to learn what you know about the Templars, we must play it safe. After all, we have no idea how far they are willing to go, so I think it best that we prepare for the worst."

Holmes then left us and perhaps five minutes later we saw him approaching from Melcombe Street and strolling leisurely toward Park Road. He was stopping and chatting with shopkeepers and teasing the children who were playing on the sidewalk. It was a delightful May morning – the sun was shining and all seemed well with the world. However, my association with Holmes had taught me that appearances can be deceiving. Perhaps ten minutes later, I saw Holmes returning in our direction from Park Road. I looked at my watch and realized it was time to leave. Donning our coats and hats, we descended the stairs and as we passed through the kitchen where Mrs. Hudson was baking something that smelled wonderful, she shook her head at us. That simple gesture conveyed her displeasure, but to her credit, she never uttered a word of protest.

We walked down the alley toward Park Row and when we emerged, I followed one of Holmes's old dictums and took the third cab that came along. Perhaps thirty minutes later, we arrived at the Northumberland. After registering, we were shown to a room on the second floor.

With nothing to do but wait for Holmes, I asked Green to tell me about the Knights Templar. Although I had become somewhat familiar with their history, I thought Green might provide even more insight with regard to these fighting monks – whose vows of chastity he maintained were as much honoured as they were ignored.

"Like so many other things in life, it all comes down to the individual," he explained. "As a result, there were any number of women who exerted influence within the group. Although they could not become members – and there may be instances in Spain during the *Reconquista* where even that rule appears to have been overlooked at times – the widows and mothers of some of the warriors wielded considerable power. All one has to do is think of Eleanor of Aquitaine in the 13th rather than the 12th century."

He spoke with passion about the Templars and was able to answer most of my questions. Before I knew it, several hours had passed.

Since Holmes had instructed us to remain in the room, we had the hotel send up lunch and we were just finishing with coffee when there was a soft knock on the door.

"Who is it?" I asked.

"It is I, Watson."

I opened the door to find Holmes standing before me in normal clothing rather than in one of his disguises.

"I don't believe you were followed to Baker Street, Captain Green. I remained on 'patrol' for another two hours. There were strangers loitering about but no one, as far as I could tell, was monitoring the comings and goings of 221B."

"And what exactly does that mean?"

"It may mean several things," Holmes replied. "The most obvious being that they, whoever they might be, are unaware of your whereabouts at present. To my way of thinking, that affords us a distinct advantage. Less likely, but still possible, is that they do not know what you look like. That too may prove to be an asset to our cause."

"I'm not certain I follow that bit of logic," said the captain.

Ignoring him, Holmes continued, "However, our biggest strength rests in the fact that they do not know we have spoken."

"You expect the woman to return to check on your progress," I exclaimed.

"I must admit that I shall be quite disappointed if she doesn't. However, this time we will be ready for her." With that pronouncement, Holmes allowed himself a small grin – it was a look that I knew boded ill for those who dared to match wits with him.

"Holmes, you can't take a woman prisoner and interrogate her when she has committed no crime," I cautioned.

"No crime?" he chuckled. "I should think that impersonating Captain Green's daughter might be considered illegal."

"Yes, but it would come down to a case of she said-they said. I will be accused of siding with you as I could hardly be considered an unbiased witness. And she could always claim that there was a misunderstanding or some sort or that you weren't paying close attention during her recitation. Either way, it's not a desirable position in which to place yourself."

"Although it pains me to say so, there is merit in what you say, Watson. I shall have to give this some serious thought."

With that, I half expected Holmes to throw himself into one of the chairs, charge his pipe and begin filling the room with the malodorous fumes of his shag. So you can imagine my surprise when Holmes turned around and said, "Captain Green, I want you to remain in your room until you hear from us. I realize it is a serious inconvenience, but your freedom – perhaps your life – may depend upon your following my instructions to the letter.

"I have no idea why these people are seeking you although I am certain it is tied to your research into the Templars. Perhaps their intentions are benign although, given the ruse employed by the young woman claiming to be your daughter, I am inclined to doubt it."

"For how long?" asked Green. "I am quite capable of taking care of myself – of that I can assure you."

"I am certain you are," replied Holmes, "in a fair fight. But these are not gentlemen concerned about fairness and good sportsmanship. I have no doubt that you would be outnumbered four or five to one and as soon as possible a gun would be clapped to your head. It would then be just a question of how much pain you could endure before they broke you.

"Early tomorrow morning, I want you to leave here, take the third cab that comes along, and register at the Langham under the name Enoch Drebber. The next few days you are to follow the same routine. After the Langham, take a room at Brown's and register as John Rance and then at Claridge's as Jonathan Small. Hopefully by then, we will have more of an idea of what our opponents are planning. But until then …" Holmes let the words trail off as he went to the writing desk and sat there scribbling on a piece of paper for a few minutes. Finally, he turned and handed it to Green. "That is a list of 10 hotels with an alias you are to use at each one."

"Do you really think all this rigmarole is necessary?" he protested.

"Unfortunately, yes. You alone know the value of your secrets, but I have to believe they are considerable."

"They are, indeed."

"Well, trust me when I say, I have seen good men do terrible things for far less than the stakes for which you appear to be playing," Holmes assured him.

"And you, Mr. Holmes. What are you playing for?"

"I play the game for its own sake, but rest assured I am always on the side of justice. Now do we have an understanding?"

With a face filled with remorse and a hint of frustration, Green nodded.

"Excellent," replied Holmes. "Rest assured that Dr. Watson or I will be in touch daily. Remember, you alone possess the knowledge they seek, so your safety is paramount."

On the way back to Baker Street, I said, "Holmes, I am rather surprised at you. It is your custom to demand complete honesty from your clients before you take their case. By his own admission, Green is holding something back, so why involve yourself?'

He smiled at me and said, "You miss one salient point, Watson."

"Oh?"

"Green is not my client. Besides I have a pretty fair idea of what he is so reluctant to share with us." Having said that, Holmes lapsed into one of his contemplative moods. I thought I was going to have to rouse him when we arrived, but he stirred and gathered himself as we pulled up to the door.

After we had taken our places in front of the fire, Holmes said, "I do apologize, Watson, but this case has me at odds and ends. We have clues aplenty – but who can say what they mean or where they lead? We have a client of sorts, for I have not been formally engaged nor have I received a retainer, who is not totally forthcoming. Normally, as you point out, I would dismiss him out of hand, but I am certain that Green has no idea what he's up against." He paused then continued, "Truth be told, neither do I, but every fibre of my being cries out that these people mean Green no good."

The rest of the day and the next two, we fell into a routine. Holmes would go out – each time in disguise – trying to learn more about the mysterious woman and the group that seemed determined to locate Captain Green. For my part, I visited Green for several hours every day at the different hotels – often leaving Baker Street through the tradesmen's entrance and always varying my routes and modes of transport as per Holmes' instructions.

Green told me that if he could only get to the British Museum and the library, he might be able to shed some light on our adversaries. However, I cautioned against such a move and offered to visit the library in his stead and bring back such volumes as he requested.

On the afternoon of the third day, I was just about to enter our rooms having returned from a morning and luncheon spent with Green in his room at Claridge's, when a cab pulled up and Holmes alighted. As he glanced around the street, the look on his face spoke volumes, so I held my tongue. However, when we entered, Mrs. Hudson came bustling out of her kitchen. "This note arrived while you were out, Mr. Holmes. It was delivered by messenger."

Taking the missive, Holmes thrust it into his coat pocket, thanked our landlady, asked if she might bring up a pot of coffee and then ascended the stairs.

Holmes doffed his coat, hanging it on the rack, disappeared into his bedroom and returned in his blue dressing gown. He then charged and lit his oily clay pipe and settled into his chair. I watched all this amazed. Finally, after I had settled myself, I asked him, "Aren't you even going to read it?"

"Read what?"

"The note Mrs. Hudson gave you; it came by messenger, so I would think it might be important."

"This Templar case demands my full attention. It is as singular a series of events as I can ever recall."

"I agree; it is unusual but still…"

"Watson, your grand gift of silence is failing you today. Since it interests you so much, why don't you read it and tell me what it says."

"I shall do that very thing," I informed him. Having said that. I went to his coat and extracted the note.

In an attempt to emulate Holmes, I noticed that the paper was of excellent quality, and that the address –

Sherlock Holmes, 221B Baker Street, Marylebone – had been typed rather than written.

I extracted a single sheet of note paper, which I read and I was so taken aback by what it said that I had to peruse it a second time. Finally, I said, "Holmes, I think you may want to have a look at this."

"I do hope this is *important*, Watson," he complained, emphasizing the word important.

I handed him the note and watched the expression on his face change from annoyance to puzzlement to amusement. "You have to give them credit, old man. They are bold."

"What do you make of it?"

"Obviously, it's a fraud. Quite frankly, I expected something like this sooner rather than later. It's most certainly a trap of some sort. But we shall keep the appointment. Now, I have to run out for a bit and attend to a few things. I shall meet you back here at five. I'd suggest you eat an early supper as it may well be a long night."

With that, Holmes threw the note in my direction. Once again, I picked it up and read it over carefully, looking for even a hint of a clue. The note was brief and to the point.

\

Dear Mr. Holmes,

I understand that you have been making inquiries about me. As you might suspect, I fear for my life. If you would be so kind as to meet me on the Hyde Park side of the Serpentine Bridge tonight at 10, I will be eternally in your debt and answer all questions you might put to me. Please come alone.

Sincerely yours.

Capt. Richard Green

Chapter 8

"You can't seriously think about keeping such an appointment," I exclaimed as he headed for the door. "Who knows what they might have planned for you?"

"Your concern is touching, Watson, and I will admit that my first instinct was to remain here and hope they sent another messenger whom we might follow. However, I am certain they would cover their tracks, so keeping this late-night rendezvous seems our best chance of advancing the case."

"If you go, I'm coming with you – and so is my sidearm."

"Well, they did say 'Please,' so I think we can safely ignore that social nicety," he laughed.

"Just tell me what it is you would like me to do."

Holmes thought for a few moments, outlined his plan and then dashed out the door and down the steps. And so it was that several hours later, I found myself "sleeping" on a park bench not too far from the entrance to the bridge on the Hyde Park side. I was dressed in what might be considered "rags" by most people. When Holmes had returned, he had pieced together my costume using bits and scraps from his various disguises. Fortunately, I was able to escape the makeup and other prosthetics that he so often employed. All I had had to do was darken my face with a bit of ash from the hearth.

I had arrived at the park at six o'clock and sat on the bench with my hat in my hands, appearing for all the world like a down-on-his luck beggar. I had even managed to collect a few pennies and one gentleman gave me two bob if I promised not to spend it on drink.

At a quarter past nine, I covered myself with newspapers and pretended to be asleep, but I was watching the bridge through slitted eyes. About half nine, three men came over the bridge from the Kensington Gardens side of the span. I heard one of the men say, "Do you think two men there will be enough?"

"I should hope so," replied the one who appeared to be their leader. "All told we are five on the ground. If Holmes gives us any trouble, we will try to capture him, but if it comes down to him or us – kill him." Although I could not place it, I thought I detected a faint trace of some sort of accent.

I shuddered at the nonchalant way he issued his orders, and I wondered how Holmes and I would fare with the odds against us.

Suddenly, one of the men spoke; he had spotted me. "What do you want to do with him?"

The leader glanced at me and said, "Let sleeping beggars lie," chuckling at his own witticism. "But if he tries to interfere…well, what's one more body?"

Just then Big Ben struck the quarter hour and the leader instructed the two men, "Okay, conceal yourselves, but if you hear me utter the phrase, 'Well, bless my soul' – then I'm counting on you to size up the situation and act accordingly."

At that, the two men took up their positions – one on either side of the bridge, concealing themselves deep in the bushes that bordered the balustrades. The apparent leader threw another glance in my direction and then stood in the middle of the entrance to the bridge perhaps a hundred feet away, holding a dark lantern that was open halfway.

When the hour sounded, no one appeared and perhaps five minutes later, one of the men from the bushes whispered, "How long are we going to wait for this bloke?"

"Be still," the leader hissed. "We cannot even be certain he received the message, so we'll wait until at least half ten."

I heard the quarter hour sound and wondered how long Holmes would make them wait. However, I need not have worried for a few minutes later, I heard my friend's voice call out, "Captain Green, is that you?"

"Now then, Mr. Holmes, it's good that you could make it as I was afraid you did not receive my message. I would have come to you at Baker Street, but I believe I am being followed."

Casting a furtive glance, I saw Holmes striding across the bridge, carrying a dark lantern of his own. It was a good thing they had those lanterns because the waning moon suddenly disappeared behind the clouds, and we found ourselves enveloped in blackness. The only discernable illumination was the dim glow emanating from the two dark lanterns.

"No, it arrived earlier today, but I didn't return to my rooms until it was nearly eight. So how may I be of service?"

"I know that my daughter came to see you a few days ago; I understand she was concerned about my disappearance."

"Yes, she asked me to make a few inquiries, and I was happy to oblige. I planned to write her tomorrow."

"Well, there's no need for that now. Did Caroline tell you anything of my research? Have you discovered anything on your own?"

"We discussed your writings and your belief that you had been given short shrift by General Warren."

"Did she happen to mention the Knights Templar?"

"Yes, yes, I believe she did."

"And have you pursued any inquiries in that direction?"

"Does it really matter?" Holmes asked innocently.

"Mr. Holmes, I believe that you and I are working at cross-purposes. I need you to tell me anything and everything you might have learned about the Templars."

I couldn't be certain because of the dark, but I imagined my friend smiling as his next remark was delivered with more than a hint of sarcasm. "I am certain that we are working at cross-purposes, sir. Unfortunately, I have no idea what ends you are pursuing."

"Mr. Holmes, I must insist that you share whatever you have learned with me? Did you discover anything on your recent trip to Royston?"

"Now what makes you think I've been to Royston?"

"Because I had you followed there. Now let's stop faffing about, shall we?

"As you wish."

"Mr. Holmes, there are forces at play far beyond your control – or mine. I am asking for your cooperation. Should you refuse my request, I am afraid I shall have to resort to other means to encourage your collaboration."

"Why don't you tell me why you are so desperate to find the real Captain Green and while you are doing that, I'll consider your request."

"I don't think you appreciate the situation, Mr. Holmes. You are in no position to bargain, so I'd suggest you tell me what I want to know."

"If you are counting on those two thugs on the other side of the bridge to provide any sort of assistance, I regret to inform you that your faith has been sorely misplaced."

"Well, bless my soul, then it's a good thing that I brought two other men with me, isn't it?"

I waited for the two ruffians whom I had watched conceal themselves to step out and confront Holmes but nothing happened.

"Did you?" inquired Holmes. "I don't see anyone."

"Well, bless my soul," he exclaimed louder, "you will soon enough."

"I don't know why you would think such a thing. Didn't your man watching my rooms report back to you the message had been delivered and that I arrived home just a few hours later?"

"So you suspected a trap?"

"Well you made it rather obvious when you signed Captain Green's name."

"I needed to make certain you'd follow the instructions in the note, and obviously you did since you are here. Based on your remarks I can only assume that you have spoken with the real Captain Green as you know I'm not he. Now let's stop chelpin' and get down to business."

"I'm still waiting for those two men of yours to appear. Perhaps you'd like to say 'Well, bless my soul' a third time and hope for the best."

Instead he asked loudly, "Where are you two?" After a pause, he continued, "I knew they were a bleedy disappointment when I hired 'em. Obviously, you had men concealed here long before I arrived. Still, Mr. Holmes, while you may think you have won this round, I wouldn't begin celebrating just yet."

"Oh? Do you have still other men who will fail to appear when you summon them? Or is that another bluff on your part?"

"I have just one other man – a sniper, a truly excellent marksman by the way who learned his craft in Her Majesty's army – and I am certain he has his sights trained on you as we speak. So you see, Mr. Holmes, I will concede this battle to you and live to fight another day." So saying, he closed his lantern and the only light I could discern was Holmes's lamp which also quickly vanished.

Suddenly a shot rang out, and I saw a spark as the bullet struck the bridge quite close to where Holmes had been standing. At that point I realized the man had not been bluffing.

Before I could ask if he were hurt, I heard Holmes yell, "Stop him if he comes your way, Watson."

I jumped off the bench and stood in the middle of the path, but I heard nothing and as far as I could tell no one had come my way.

I walked toward the bridge and suddenly, a tiny spot of light appeared. As I headed towards it, I heard Holmes whisper, "Stay back, Watson. The sniper may still be in the vicinity." Then I felt his arm around mine guiding me away from the bridge – and the light.

When we had gone some distance, Holmes produced a second lantern and left it in the middle of the path as we stepped quickly to the side. "Just in case that sniper is still in place," he explained. However, there were no more shots, and a few minutes later, two men – one of whom I recognized as Shinwell Johnson – arrived carrying their own dark lanterns. "They knew nothing, Mr. Holmes. Just hired muscle for the evening."

"And the two on the other side of the bridge?" asked Holmes.

"My men say the same thing," said Shinwell. "They were each given £5 and promised another five if they 'elped out with no questions asked."

"£5 – that's quite a sum. Where were they recruited?" Holmes asked.

"At different pubs in Whitechapel. 'Alf the blokes I knows there would kill their own mother for a few bob – let alone £10," stated Shinwell.

"True enough," said Holmes. "Unfortunately their leader escaped in the darkness. We will talk tomorrow, Shinwell." Pulling his wallet from his pocket, Holmes extracted several notes and handed them to Shinwell. "There's a little something extra for each man and yourself. Thank the men for me and tell them job well done."

Both Shinwell and the other man thanked Holmes, and then they faded back into the darkness as silently as they had come. As you can imagine, my mind was reeling with questions, and I was unable to contain my curiosity. As we walked through the darkened park, I said to Holmes, "How did you know what they had planned?"

"Believe me, Watson, when I tell you that I saw every aspect of that ambush before we had even departed from Baker Street."

"But how?"

"I simply put myself in their shoes and asked myself what would I do in a similar situation. The bridge was an ideal meeting place because once I stepped onto the span my options for escape were quite limited. I could go back, go forward or jump into the water. I anticipated his cutting off my preferred escape routes, so when I went out this afternoon, I hired Shinwell and asked him to round up three other good men.

"I must admit the sniper was a bit of a surprise, but that he would take that extra precaution speaks volumes about his deviousness and perhaps his determination. I must admit I underestimated him this time, Watson, a mistake I shan't make again."

By this time we had reached Bayswater Road and despite the late hour, we had little trouble finding a cab. Some twenty minutes later, we were stepping down in front of our rooms.

After we had ascended the stairs and settled in front of the fireplace with brandy and cigars, I turned to Holmes and said, "This whole business has taken a rather nasty turn."

"I agree, Watson, and I have no one to blame but myself. I should have insisted that Green be totally candid with us, and tomorrow I will make that crystal clear. I've been blundering around without a full appreciation of the circumstances surrounding us. It could have cost us dearly, and that situation cannot be allowed to continue."

"And if Green balks?"

"Then I will find myself compelled to drop the case. It's not something I relish doing as this affair poses any number of unusual qualities; however, I have compromised my principles once already and the results could have been catastrophic.

"Now, why don't you get some rest? I must give this problem a great deal more thought."

I bade Holmes good night and when I reached the foot of the stairs, Holmes said, "One more thing – did you notice anything unusual about their leader tonight?"

I paused, considered for a moment and then said, "I thought I detected some trace of an accent in his speech, but I could not place it. He also used a few words that were strange to me."

"So you heard them as well. Excellent. It gives me something else to consider. Now good night, Watson, and thank you. I'll see you at breakfast."

I said, "Think nothing of it," and made my way upstairs where I was sound asleep just moments after my head hit the pillow."

Chapter 9

I must admit that I was surprised to find Holmes at the breakfast table calmly drinking coffee when I came down the next morning. He often tells me he'll be somewhere and then goes off on another track entirely.

"Good morning, Watson. After you have eaten, we must go see Captain Green. We need to get to the bottom of this Templar mystery, and he is the only one who can help us."

"Where is he today?"

"He should be leaving Claridge's and checking in to the Charing Cross Hotel under the name Jonathan Small."

I had to laugh at Holmes using all the names of the characters from *A Study in Scarlet* and *The Sign of Four* as aliases for Green, but it made perfect sense. Too often people use assumed names close to their own, and Holmes was guarding against that possibility by providing Green with a list of pseudonyms that bore no resemblance whatsoever to Green's first name and surname.

We descended to Baker Street and walked outside to a brilliant blue sky. Although I suggested a leisurely walk, Holmes insisted upon a cab. "I am anxious to hear what Green has to say."

As you might expect, the cab ride was spent in silence. Charing Cross station is located in the center of the city. The hotel, which had been constructed directly above the station, was convenient for business travelers, and it offered all the latest amenities. The front desk clerk informed us that Mr. Small was staying in Room 312. We took the lift up, and when Holmes knocked, Green asked, "Who is it?"

"It is I, Mr. Small," Holmes responded. Only then did Green open the door and admit us. I could see that the constant confinement was taking a toll on the man. His complexion seemed a bit more sallow, and the energy in his walk as he had us into the sitting room was missing.

"What's the news, Mr. Holmes?" Green asked after he had poured us coffee.

Holmes then outlined everything that had transpired yesterday afternoon and last evening. When he had finished, he looked at Green and said, "Usually, I demand total honesty from my clients. After all, how can I pursue a course of action that is in their best interests if I don't know what those interests are? I am afraid I must demand that you place all the facts before me, or else I will be forced to terminate our relationship.

"The choice is entirely yours, but I think to put things in perspective you must ask yourself: Which is more important – my secrets or my life? For I suspect that if you try to pursue this alone, you may well lose both."

There was a pause, and then Holmes said softly, "If you'd like some time to think it over, Dr. Watson and I can return after lunch."

"No, no, that won't be necessary, Mr. Holmes. You have made your point and most convincingly I might add."

"You've made a wise choice," I said. "Holmes is a man of integrity and your secrets – whatever they may be – are safe with him." Saying that, I rose to leave, for I felt my presence might be an impediment to Green's forthcomingness.

However, Holmes stopped me, saying, "Please remain, Doctor. As has been the case so many times in the past, your assistance may prove invaluable in this endeavour." He then turned to Green and reassured him, "Dr. Watson is the soul of discretion. Anything you say in front of me, you may also say in front of him."

Between his enforced isolation and Holmes's forceful words, much of the fight seemed to have gone out of Green, He sighed with resignation, and said, "Let me begin at the beginning. Exactly how much do you know about the Knights Templar, Mr. Holmes?"

When Holmes replied that he knew a fair amount but obviously not as much as Green, the answer seemed to satisfy the captain. He then proceeded to give a concise but detailed history of the order, much of which has already been mentioned. I glanced over at Holmes at several points, and to my eyes his impatience was obvious. However, since he had brought this on himself, he suffered in silence.

For the sake of brevity, I will deal only with the section of Green's narrative that proved of interest to Holmes.

"As you know," he continued, sounding more like an academic than an explorer, "the Templars had amassed untold riches. King Philip coveted their treasure; no, King Philip *needed* their treasure. Other monarchs remembered the good the order had done, so while Templars were arrested all across Europe, they were not pursued with the same vigor and vitriol as the French monarch exhibited.

"My research would seem to indicate that here in England things played out quite differently. Although King Edward I had raided the Templar treasury in 1283, King Edward II initially was quite skeptical about the accusations. However, when Pope Clement intervened, Edward's hand was forced, reluctantly by all accounts, to order the Templars arrested on the 8th of January 1308. Still, only a few handsful of knights were taken into custody. Their trial, if such it can be called, was presided over by two inquisitors dispatched by the Vatican – Deodatus, the abbot of Lagny; and Sicard de Vaur. The trial did not begin until November, more than 10 months later. During that time many of the Templars roamed the country freely; a goodly number fled to Ireland and Scotland.

"From everything I have been able to learn and from the research I have conducted, the Templars could see which way the wind was blowing. Although the king had confiscated the lands and a significant portion of their treasure, there are still vast sums that remain unaccounted for.

"You don't mean…" I interrupted.

"That's exactly what I mean, Doctor. I believe that there is an enormous fortune, perhaps hundreds of thousands of pounds worth of gold and jewels that the Templars managed to conceal before they were finally taken into custody."

Green then spent another few minutes concluding his narrative. After he stopped speaking, I could only exclaim, "What an extraordinary story!"

"And sadly, Doctor, we do not know the whole story nor how it ends – yet."

Holmes who had remained silent during Green's recitation suddenly roused himself. "I agree, Watson, it is an extraordinary tale. So your research into de Molay's innocence was merely a pretext to allow you to seek out the treasure."

"I'm afraid that is true, Mr. Holmes. It started out as an attempt to prove the perfidy of the monarchs but that was proving impossible due to the destruction of so many documents, so when I came across the missing treasure, I shifted my attention to something I believed more attainable."

"And the trips to France?"

"Initially, they had a dual purpose but one soon gave way to the other. As I am sure you know there were many, many connections between England and France at that time."

"Captain Green, do you have any proof that the Templars hid portions of their treasure? As you said the king seized large portions of it. I mean surely in nearly six centuries, someone would have stumbled across chests of coins or jewels," Holmes said.

"Not necessarily, Mr. Holmes. Consider the Lewis chessmen. They were created in the 12th century but discovered only in 1834 in the sand of a bay on the island of Lewis in Scotland. In that same vein, the Alfred Jewel was fashioned in the ninth century but remained hidden until 1693 when it was unearthed by a plough in a field in North Petherton, Somerset. No one was looking for either of those, and there were no records to indicate their creation or location."

"Your point, Captain?" asked Holmes.

"I have written records which I believe indicate that vast sums were moved from various Templar treasuries and hidden in 1312 – right before the last of the Templars were finally seized in England. I can show you the ledger entries from two different Templar banks where the withdrawals were noted. As for records indicating where the money was taken and stored they has proved devilishly difficult to find, but I believe I am making some small progress in that area."

"I am certain you are," replied Holmes, "else why the attempts to locate you – and unless I miss my guess – imprison you? Are you working alone in this endeavour?"

"I have two people assisting me – a linguist and a historian – however they know nothing about the treasure as of yet. They are working – as you are, Mr. Holmes – because the work is its own reward."

I had to smile when Green used Holmes' own words against him. However, I will admit that Holmes took it well and simply said, "A touch, Captain Green. A definite touch."

With that, the tension in the room dissipated, and it was finally understood that we were all on the same side. Holmes then asked, "The records of the two Templar banks – which ones were they?"

"The first set of notes was discovered in one of the barns at Cressing Temple in Essex. As I'm sure you are aware, Cressing Temple was one of the earliest and largest Templar estates in England. After a series of unsuccessful searches at other Templar sites, I came across a second set of notes, eerily similar to the first, in Baldock in Hertfordshire. In the first half of the 13th century, that location was the Templar headquarters in England. Beneath

Hertford, there is a veritable warren of tunnels with Hertford Castle at its center. I should also add that in 1309, four knights from Temple Dinsley near Hitchin were imprisoned by King Edward II. Their crime? He believed they were concealing a lost treasure. I don't know about you, Mr. Holmes, but I am not one to believe in coincidences."

I said nothing but smiled to myself as I recalled Holmes had on more than one occasion expressed that exact same sentiment.

"If you have these notes, why haven't you acted upon them?" asked Holmes.

"The problem is that while some of the notes are straightforward, having been written in Latin, there are other parts that appear to have been written in some sort of secret writing. You may not be aware of this, Mr. Holmes, but the Templars had developed their own code using pieces of the Maltese Cross to represent the various letters of the alphabet."

"Yes," replied Homes drily, "I have undertaken a study of various codes and secret writings. The Templar Code is simply a substitution encryption system – quite similar to the Pigpen and Rosicrucian ciphers. Once you have the key, they are quite simple to decode, but even without the key, if you have a large enough sample, they can eventually be conquered."

"That was my thought as well, Mr. Holmes, but although I have laboured over these messages for a great many hours, their secret continues to elude me."

"And the linguist and historian you have employed, what progress have they made?"

"I am afraid they are as baffled as I; however, they both toiled at it for several weeks and then admitted defeat."

"I should like to have a look at the documents," said Holmes. "Perhaps a set of fresh eyes can bring a new perspective to the problem."

"I can only wish you well, Mr. Holmes. I freely admit myself overmatched."

I saw the slight smile on Holmes's face, and I knew that he was up for the challenge. If it were possible to feel pity for an inanimate object, I would have felt sorry for that code. There was no doubt in my mind that it would yield its secrets – albeit unwillingly – to my friend's razor-sharp intellect.

"Where are the codes now?" asked Holmes.

"I have concealed the originals in my home in Roystan."

"Then I think it would behoove us to go and retrieve them at once before they fall into the hands of our foes."

"There's no need for concern there," remarked Green. "Even if they were to be found, I have the sequences committed to memory and could easily put pen to paper and re-create them."

I knew that Holmes trusted only his own intellect in such matters, so I wasn't surprised when he said, "Still, I should like to see them for myself. You never know what other information might be gleaned from the paper, the ink and the manner in which the symbols were composed."

We then decided that we should all travel to Royston together. As there were no trains from Charing Cross to Roystan, we hailed a cab and headed for Covent Garden station. We arrived about ten minutes later and after a short wait boarded the 11:42 to Roystan. Perhaps an hour later we alighted in Roystan and after hailing a cab, we headed directly for Captain Green's house which was located just a few miles outside the town.

He lived in a rather large red brick house that would not have looked out of place in St. James Wood. He must have seen the look on my face because he said, "The house belonged to my wife's parents. It came to her when they died, and I inherited it when she passed. I lived here with my daughter until her accident, and since then I have spent far less time here as it seemed less like a home than a constant reminder of my losses. Fortunately, my work and research have led to me being abroad for weeks and months at a time."

All I could do was nod sympathetically. As we descended from the cab, Holmes turned and said quietly, "We may not be alone here."

At that point I finally noticed that the front door was slightly ajar. Green had seen it as well and said, "I'm certain I locked that door when I left."

Holmes then began to examine the ground. Finally, he stood up and smiled. Pointing, he said, "Those are the ruts that were made by the wheels of our cab. If you look carefully, you can see the wheel marks left by a dog cart. Here is where they arrived and here is where the cab stood while it waited. You can see the marks are much less deep, and finally you can see the deeper ruts when they departed."

"Any idea when they were here?" I asked.

"Within the past week. We've had no rain for the past several days and the marks are quite well preserved, so I should say sometime shortly after the last rain, which was Wednesday I believe."

Having made his pronouncement, Holmes led us quietly to the front door. Pushing it open, he yelled, "Hello, is anyone at home?"

When no answer was forthcoming, he said, "There may be someone in hiding but I suspect not. Captain, would you take us to where you kept the papers."

Green then led us down a darkened hallway and opened a door. We followed him into the room which was almost pitch black and I nearly tripped over something on the floor. By that time, Green had reached the French doors and drawn back the heavy curtains. Even in the grey light of the overcast day, it was easy to see that someone had thoroughly searched the room and they had spared nothing. The floor was littered with books and papers, the leather couch and chairs had been slit open and overturned and much of the stuffing had joined the books on the floor. Everything had been removed from the walls and lie among the items on the floor. I spotted what I believed to be a Templar shield as well as two broadswords among the debris. The desk had been overturned and even the legs of the small sideboard had been broken as if someone were checking to see if they had been hollowed out.

Holmes moved to the desk, righted it and lit a lamp. In the brighter light we could see that the damage was considerable.

"Oh dear," said Green. "I never thought it would come to this."

"I did try to warn you, Captain. These are dangerous men who will apparently stop at nothing to get their hands on that Templar treasure."

Green who had been glancing around the room seemed satisfied with the sight that greeted him. In fact, I thought a saw a hint of a brief smile flash across his features but I couldn't be sure as his face was half turned away, facing the windows.

Suddenly he faced us and said, "Well, I think I can say with reasonable certainty that their search was unsuccessful."

"What makes you say that?" I asked.

"Because the item in which I concealed them is exactly where I left it."

"Well that's good news!" I exclaimed, glancing about the room in an effort to discover the hidden documents.

"Care to hazard a guess as to where the papers are concealed, Mr. Holmes?" asked Green.

Chapter 10

Holmes smiled and said, "I can only hope the rest of the case falls into place as easily as that."

"I should like to hear your guess, Mr. Holmes," Green repeated.

A pained look passed across my friend's features, and he glanced at me before turning to Green and saying, "I never guess, Captain Green. I regard it as a shocking habit destructive to the logical faculty."

"Then where are my notes, Mr. Holmes?"

With that Holmes pulled a chair over to the window and stepping gingerly upon the slashed leather, he reached up and removed the rod holding the curtains from its mountings above the French doors. Descending from the chair and handing it to Green, he said, "I'm assuming you slid them in from the right, but as you may have taken other precautions, I'll let you retrieve them lest I damage them in some way."

"Bravo, Mr. Holmes," said Green who was quite obviously impressed. "The descriptions of your deductive abilities do not even begin to do you justice. But tell me, how did you gu–, I mean know?"

"It's rather obvious. All of the items in the room have been moved and searched – quite thoroughly I might

94

add. Now, the only things that appear to have been untouched were the curtains and the rod on which they hang. I also noticed that on two different occasions you cast rather furtive glances at the top of the curtains. I trust that the rest of the chain is rather self-explanatory."

I chuckled to myself at Holmes's rather subtle rebuke, but I was quickly taken aback when I heard Green suddenly utter a profanity. He had unscrewed a rather elaborate endcap from the rod and withdrawn a sheaf of papers; however, it was obvious that something was badly amiss.

"What's wrong?" inquired Holmes.

"These are not my papers. Somehow they found the papers and took them. They left this note to taunt me apparently." With that he thrust a sheet of paper towards Holmes. He took it, read it over and then passed it to me. In a neat script, the note read:

Dear Captain Green,

I must congratulate you on selecting a very clever hiding place for the documents. As you can see by the state of the room, it took us quite some time to locate them. Were you expecting to find them safe and sound since the curtains appeared untouched? If so, I am sorry to disappoint you.

Thus far you and Mr. Holmes have caused me a great deal of unnecessary aggravation, so I must insist that you and he cease and desist at once.

We have the code; the game is over, so do be a good sport and throw in the towel.

Seneschal,

Temple Yorkshire

After reading this remarkable document, I turned to Holmes and asked "What do you make of this? And what exactly is a seneschal?"

Both Holmes and Green started to speak at once, but Holmes stopped and deferred to the historian. Green began, "As I am sure you know, the leader of the Knights Templar was the Grand Master. Each Grand Master would choose a Seneschal or Grand Commander. He would be the right hand of the Master, and he would be the individual responsible for administering all the lands belonging to the local temple. He would also be tasked with handling all war matters such as feeding and moving the armies."

"Well, if this letter is signed the 'Seneschal, Temple Yorkshire,' it would seem that we are up against a group of men who see themselves as modern-day Templars," I said.

"So it would appear," said Holmes, "but I need not remind you appearances can be deceiving. You may have summed it up perfectly, Watson, or we may dealing with a group of men who want us to think they are some sort of contemporary Templars. Obviously, we cannot say for certain which is true at this time although I do have my suspicions.

"Captain, you had said you memorized the messages just in case they were ever damaged or lost. Might I trouble you to reproduce them now?"

"Of course, Mr. Holmes." Righting another chair and pulling it to the desk, Green then rooted around looking for something with which to write. Finally, he gave up and with a rueful smile asked, "Do either of you gentlemen have a pen?"

As a physician, I always carry a pen just in case I should suddenly need to write a prescription. I handed it to him and he thanked me and set to work. A few minutes later, he handed Holmes a sheet of paper. "That is the sticking point, Mr. Holmes. All the other messages were written in Latin and rather easy to decipher, but this one had been written in the code of the Templars, and it was sealed with wax on which the Templar insignia had been imprinted. As a result, I am inclined to think it a bit more important than the others."

"I quite agree," said Holmes, "and was the wax unbroken when you found the letter?"

"It was, which is what makes me think the treasure might still be there if we can only solve this cipher."

"What do you think, Watson?" asked Holmes handing me the paper. "This shouldn't be too difficult to crack although a larger sample size would certainly make matters easier. Still…" and he let the words trail off.

I looked at the paper and was rather stunned to discover a series of symbols whose meaning, as you might expect, eluded me entirely.

$$\wedge \vee > \times \Diamond \vee \Diamond \Diamond \quad \Diamond \vee \triangleright \times \triangleleft$$

"I don't quite know what to make of it, Holmes."

"It's obviously a substitution code. Given that it was based on Latin, our lives are just a little bit easier."

"How so?" I asked.

"The letter J only began to appear in the 16th century, up until then the letter I did double-duty. As a result, we are working with an alphabet of 25 letters. It's a small thing, but nonetheless, it does reduce the number of variables with which we have to contend."

"Mr. Holmes, what is my role going forward?" asked Green.

"That remains to be seen, Captain. Until I can make some headway with this cipher, I think that you can return to your normal life. Since they now have what they wanted from you, I am inclined to think the danger has passed you by."

"But I should like to stay involved with the investigation. You never know when my expertise about the Templars may prove useful."

I thought Green made a valid point and was about to say so, when Holmes said, "I understand your feelings, and I quite agree. Do you have a friend or family member in London with whom you could visit for a while? After all, we will be operating from there rather than Roystan – at least for the foreseeable future."

"I could stay with Lieutenant Foster; I served with him in the army in Jerusalem, and he and I have remained good friends. He lives in Mayfair, not too far from you and Dr. Watson."

"Excellent! There are times when I could use a second set of eyes to help in my research. Normally, I rely on Watson, but his practice seems to demand more and more of his time of late."

"Wonderful!" he exclaimed. He then wrote on a sheet of paper and handed it to Holmes. "This is Foster's address; you should be able to reach me there in a day or two."

I looked at him quizzically and he must have seen the look on my face. "I need to make arrangements to have this place tidied up." Turning to Holmes, he said, "You don't think I should hire a watchman, do you?"

"I don't think that will be necessary. Just secure your valuables, have a new lock installed on your front door and perhaps ask a neighbour or two to look in on the place every now and then. When you tell them you were burgled, I guarantee they will look after your property and be a bit more careful with their own."

"Thank you, Mr. Holmes," said Green. "I suppose you and Dr. Watson will be returning to London now?"

"That is my intent. You say you have spent considerable time on this code?"

"I have – I can't tell you how many hours."

"Well, I can only assume that it is going to take me some time as well, and the sooner I get to it, the sooner I can solve this enigma."

"Shall I call on you when I arrive in London?"

"It's always best to send a messenger and set up a specific time to meet. Watson and I keep what what can best be described as irregular hours."

Green joined us in the cab ride to the station where we bid him farewell. He was going to need the cab to contact workers as well as his neighbours.

The train ride to London was spent mostly in silence. At one point, I summoned up my courage and asked Holmes, "Do you really think you can break the code where three others have failed?"

Holmes gave me a rather withering look and said, "You may recall, Watson, that I have penned a rather trifling monograph upon the subject of all forms of secret writings and ciphers in which I analyse no fewer than one hundred and sixty separate ciphers. I should hope that a code composed by a group of monks in the Middle Ages is not able to outwit me." After that pronouncement he lapsed back into silence as did I.

For the sake of brevity, I will simply sum up the next three days in as concise a fashion as I possibly can. No sooner had we arrived at Baker Street than Holmes changed into his dressing gown, charged his pipe, lit it with an ember from the fire and settled himself in front of the hearth with the coded message Green had given him along with several pencils and a small pile of foolscap.

As you might expect, he shunned dinner and sat there trying to break the code, and he continued in this fashion for the better part of the next few days. The only nourishment, if such it can be called, which he allowed himself was coffee and an occasional biscuit, and although

I was often out, I am inclined to think that he drank a prodigious amount of coffee.

Each morning I would leave for Barts and each evening I would return home to find the pile of foolscap on the floor had grown. Holmes was so immersed in his work that on at least three occasions he ran out of tobacco and had to send out for more. He was smoking so much, that anyone entering the room might have thought he had wandered onto a fog-shrouded moor.

All this while, Holmes was growing increasingly irritable until finally early in the evening of the third day he threw his hands up in frustration and said, "I hate to admit it, Watson, but this code appears to have bested me."

As you might imagine I was stunned to hear such an admission from my friend. "What seems to be the difficulty?"

"The Templar code is but 25 symbols; ordinarily, this would take me no more than an hour or two to break."

"Really? I would have thought even for one as experienced as you, it would require some time."

"Ordinarily, you would be right but years ago, I constructed a Vigenere Table, sometimes called a double-entry table."

He then showed me a large piece of paper on which the alphabet had been printed across the top and down the side while the rest of the sheet was filled with various permutations of the letters. I have reproduced it here:

	A	B	C	D	E	F	G	H	I	J	K	L	M	N	O	P	Q	R	S	T	U	V	W	X	Y	Z
A	A	B	C	D	E	F	G	H	I	J	K	L	M	N	O	P	Q	R	S	T	U	V	W	X	Y	Z
B	B	C	D	E	F	G	H	I	J	K	L	M	N	O	P	Q	R	S	T	U	V	W	X	Y	Z	A
C	C	D	E	F	G	H	I	J	K	L	M	N	O	P	Q	R	S	T	U	V	W	X	Y	Z	A	B
D	D	E	F	G	H	I	J	K	L	M	N	O	P	Q	R	S	T	U	V	W	X	Y	Z	A	B	C
E	E	F	G	H	I	J	K	L	M	N	O	P	Q	R	S	T	U	V	W	X	Y	Z	A	B	C	D
F	F	G	H	I	J	K	L	M	N	O	P	Q	R	S	T	U	V	W	X	Y	Z	A	B	C	D	E
G	G	H	I	J	K	L	M	N	O	P	Q	R	S	T	U	V	W	X	Y	Z	A	B	C	D	E	F
H	H	I	J	K	L	M	N	O	P	Q	R	S	T	U	V	W	X	Y	Z	A	B	C	D	E	F	G
I	I	J	K	L	M	N	O	P	Q	R	S	T	U	V	W	X	Y	Z	A	B	C	D	E	F	G	H
J	J	K	L	M	N	O	P	Q	R	S	T	U	V	W	X	Y	Z	A	B	C	D	E	F	G	H	I
K	K	L	M	N	O	P	Q	R	S	T	U	V	W	X	Y	Z	A	B	C	D	E	F	G	H	I	J
L	L	M	N	O	P	Q	R	S	T	U	V	W	X	Y	Z	A	B	C	D	E	F	G	H	I	J	K
M	M	N	O	P	Q	R	S	T	U	V	W	X	Y	Z	A	B	C	D	E	F	G	H	I	J	K	L
N	N	O	P	Q	R	S	T	U	V	W	X	Y	Z	A	B	C	D	E	F	G	H	I	J	K	L	M
O	O	P	Q	R	S	T	U	V	W	X	Y	Z	A	B	C	D	E	F	G	H	I	J	K	L	M	N
P	P	Q	R	S	T	U	V	W	X	Y	Z	A	B	C	D	E	F	G	H	I	J	K	L	M	N	O
Q	Q	R	S	T	U	V	W	X	Y	Z	A	B	C	D	E	F	G	H	I	J	K	L	M	N	O	P
R	R	S	T	U	V	W	X	Y	Z	A	B	C	D	E	F	G	H	I	J	K	L	M	N	O	P	Q
S	S	T	U	V	W	X	Y	Z	A	B	C	D	E	F	G	H	I	J	K	L	M	N	O	P	Q	R
T	T	U	V	W	X	Y	Z	A	B	C	D	E	F	G	H	I	J	K	L	M	N	O	P	Q	R	S
U	U	V	W	X	Y	Z	A	B	C	D	E	F	G	H	I	J	K	L	M	N	O	P	Q	R	S	T
V	V	W	X	Y	Z	A	B	C	D	E	F	G	H	I	J	K	L	M	N	O	P	Q	R	S	T	U
W	W	X	Y	Z	A	B	C	D	E	F	G	H	I	J	K	L	M	N	O	P	Q	R	S	T	U	V
X	X	Y	Z	A	B	C	D	E	F	G	H	I	J	K	L	M	N	O	P	Q	R	S	T	U	V	W
Y	Y	Z	A	B	C	D	E	F	G	H	I	J	K	L	M	N	O	P	Q	R	S	T	U	V	W	X
Z	Z	A	B	C	D	E	F	G	H	I	J	K	L	M	N	O	P	Q	R	S	T	U	V	W	X	Y

"The idea," Holmes explained, "is that any letter can be represented by any other letter. Let us say your message is HOLMES and the key word is WATSON. You go to the H in the top row and then down to the W row on the side and we have the letter D. Then you would go to the O on the top and the A on the side and you have O. When you have finished, your coded message would read DOEESF."

"My word, that's clever, but if you know how it works I fail to see the problem."

"You don't know clever, Watson, The Vigenere Cipher wasn't invented until almost two centuries after the order was disbanded, so not only were the Templars ahead of their time in banking but in coding as well. As I said, they obviously employed a key but the other variable that makes the cipher so difficult is adding yet a second variable. You can set up your code and then both the coder and recipient agree on a number – either positive or negative. So if you agreed that DOG was the key, if you made it plus three, the first letter is really G and if it's a negative three, the first letter is A. And that would follow suit for the rest of the key and the code."

"And if you wanted to complicate matters even more, you could make a sentence or phrase the key so that it is constantly changing although there obviously will be some overlap when letters repeat."

"And is there no way to solve it then?"

"There is one possibility that I can still explore."

"Oh?"

"Have you ever heard of Charles Babbage?"

"The name rings a bell – something to do with mathematics if I am remembering correctly."

"You are indeed, old man. More than sixty years ago, Mister Babbage developed what he called a 'Difference Engine.' It is a machine capable of calculating mathematical tables, albeit in a somewhat limited fashion. When that project stalled, he came up with a new idea which he dubbed the 'Analytical Engine.' He received some funding from the government, but the project ended up proving quite costly, and I'm told the machine had reached a weight in excess of four tons when the funds were finally cut off.

"His son, Henry, has continued the work, and he and his cohorts are making progress from what I understand. Fortunately, when I attended university there was a fellow there, a lecturer in mathematics, who is now working with Henry to advance the idea and see it to completion. I wonder if he might be able to assist us with breaking this code."

"It certainly sounds like an idea worth exploring, and if it will get you out of these stuffy rooms, I'm all for it."

"Excellent. We shall call upon Mr. Imp tomorrow. He's quite a brilliant fellow with numbers as I recall, and we always got along."

"In the meantime, Holmes, might we open a window or two?"

The next morning we took a cab to the Limehouse Basin, and Holmes was soon knocking on the door of a rather inauspicious looking warehouse. It was answered by a thin lanky man, perhaps in height the same as Holmes, who carried his years well. He greeted my friend warmly, "Sherlock Holmes, I haven't seen you in, what has it been, fifteen, no, eighteen years! Yet you look exactly the same, and I see that you made good on creating your own profession. Bravo!"

"Watson, allow me to introduce Mr. Steven Imp, or is it Dr. Imp now?"

"I did succeed in passing my doctoral examinations some years ago, but Steve is fine. I was never one to stand on formality. By the way, Dr. Watson, I must confess to looking forward to your recounting of Holmes's adventures each month in *The Strand.*"

We shook hands, and I was impressed by his strong grip and piercing blue eyes that hinted at an inner intelligence.

"How can I be of assistance?" he asked Holmes.

Holmes quickly summarized the problem and said, "Anything you can do would be a tremendous help." He then handed him a copy of the symbols.

"Well, it's rather short which is certainly to our advantage; still, given the machine's limitations at present, I shall have to run it in two batches, but I think the new and improved Analytical Engine should be able to handle this without too much difficulty. I'd love to introduce you to Henry Babbage – he's also a big admirer – but he is in America at present trying to interest one of their universities, Harvard, I believe, in partnering with us."

"Might I see your machine?" I asked.

"Certainly," replied Imp, who then led us into a large room at the rear of the warehouse. While there were a few desks along the walls, the room was dominated by a single machine which stood about ten feet tall and perhaps twenty-five long. It was about the same size as a small locomotive.

"My word!" I exclaimed.

"Yes, it's quite something, isn't it? This one is perhaps twice as large as its predecessor the Difference Engine. Now we are at work trying to reduce its size which has proven no easy task."

Holmes, who seemed singularly unimpressed by the mechanical behemoth before him, asked, "Do you have any idea how long it will take?"

"Running the machine itself won't take very long; it's preparing the cards that consumes the most time. If you could come back tomorrow afternoon, I am pretty certain I may have something for you."

Holmes thanked the scientist, and we headed home. "Well, that certainly sounds promising," I said.

"Indeed it does, but I must admit that the notion of a machine outthinking a human being is more than a bit unnerving."

"Holmes, as you well know, machines are already stronger, faster and more durable than men. Consider the locomotive or the steamboat or the power loom. All of those and more are capable of surpassing what men can do. The important thing to remember is that we invented them and we control them.

"Now, this Analytical Engine can do only mathematics, something most people struggle with anyway – so in that sense it will be another boon to mankind. Besides, I'm sure that there will never be machines that are smarter than men. I'd suggest we best leave those notions to Messers Wells and Verne."

"Still, I can't help but worry…" and then Holmes let the words trail off.

I knew he would not be dissuaded, and I saw no point in continuing the discussion.

When we arrived home, Mrs. Hudson came up to our rooms. She knocked on the door and Holmes bade her enter. She handed him a note and said, "This arrived by messenger shortly after you left this morning."

Holmes thanked her and then examined the envelope. "High-quality paper and the type used to address the envelope seems familiar. Slitting the envelope open with a penknife, he extracted a single piece of paper. He read it, re-read it and then chuckled before re-reading it a third time.

"What on Earth does it say?"

Holmes then handed me the letter. The top contained a paragraph written in cursive followed by a row symbols of from the Templar alphabet. It concluded with another two sentences in cursive and the closing.

Dear Mr. Holmes,

> *If you can translate this, perhaps it is time we brought our animosity to a cessation and pooled our resources and knowledge. As the old saying goes: Half a loaf is better than none.*

If interested please respond in the agony column of the Daily Mail. I understand that is your preferred method of communication.

Seneschal,

Temple Yorkshire

"Can you translate it, Holmes?"

"Just give me a minute, old man," With that he fetched pen and paper and his Vigenere Cipher key, sat down at the breakfast table and began scratching away. A few minutes later, he chuckled and said, "It appears we may have stolen a march on our adversaries, Watson."

"Why? What does it say?"

"Unless I am totally incorrect, something I am inclined to doubt, the message translates to: 'It appears we have reached an impasse.' Obviously, they have been unable to break the code. If they had, I am certain they would have sent me a message that I could not decipher just to tweak me. They are using the symbols of the Templar code in the simplest substitution possible. However, if the Analytical Engine can ascertain the meaning of these symbols, we will be that much further ahead of our antagonists."

"I understand that we possess information that our adversaries lack, but I am unclear as to how we can turn that to our advantage."

110

"Really? Do give it some thought, Watson. In the meantime, we will just have to wait to see what tomorrow brings."

Chapter 11

The next morning over breakfast I noticed that Holmes had resumed his habit of perusing the papers – something he had eschewed while trying to crack the code. Despite his misgivings, I sensed that he had come to believe in the power of the Analytical Engine, and all I could hope was that his faith had not been misplaced.

I had taken the day off from Barts as I wanted to be with Holmes when he found out whether Imp and the Analytical Engine had been successful. It was shortly after ten that I heard the front door bell ring and a few minutes later, there was a knock on the door. "Come in, Lestrade," yelled Holmes.

The door opened, and Inspector Lestrade entered the room. I could tell by the expression on his face that he was tired and worried. "Coffee, Inspector?" I asked.

"Yes, Doctor, that would be much appreciated. It has been a rather trying morning."

"What can I do for you today, Inspector?" asked Holmes.

"I know that you are familiar with the holdings of the Wallace Collection."

"I can only assume that you have been speaking with Mr. Rotondo."

"Indeed, we were summoned there early this morning. It seems the place was broken into last night."

"Oh?" said Holmes, the picture of innocence.

"A number of items were taken from one of their exhibit rooms."

"And were said items all related to the Knights Templar in some way?"

"I'm fairly certain you know they were," said Lestrade. "Two questions, Mr. Holmes?"

"Only two, Inspector?"

"For the moment," growled Lestrade. "First, what are we to make of this theft, and second, what else do you know?"

"I had hoped to avoid involving the official force," said Holmes, "as no real crime – outside of breaking and entering – had been committed. However, since our adversaries appear to have crossed that Rubicon, I suppose you might as well know everything."

With that Holmes offered a brief version of the events that had led up to the theft, omitting a number of details – some for obvious reasons. When he had finished, I could see a look of deep concern on Lestrade's face. "So you're telling me that this involves some sort of treasure from the Middle Ages and a group of individuals who see themselves as the heirs to the Knights Templar?"

"I don't think I could have summed it up better myself, Inspector, although I am certain that when Watson gets around to chronicling this adventure, that summary may find itself embellished so as to be far less succinct but far more romantic."

Lestrade smiled in spite of himself as did I, but then we all turned serious again. "So what is your next move, Mr. Holmes?"

Holmes replied, "I have an appointment to keep this afternoon, and after that things are uncertain. Perhaps we can meet again tomorrow morning. Shall I tell Mrs. Hudson to set an extra plate for breakfast?"

"I'll see you at eight," replied Lestrade, "and in the meantime I'll make a few discreet inquiries about these knights errant."

After Lestrade had departed, I said, "That went well."

"Indeed," said Holmes, "I expected the inspector to be far more reticent about rendering aid and comfort; still, let's not look a gift horse."

After lunch, we hailed a cab and headed back to the docks. When we knocked on the door, Imp greeted us and I could tell by the smile on his face that he had good news for Holmes.

"I'm assuming by the grin you're sporting that all went well," I said.

"Indeed, Dr. Watson, the machine proved its mettle once again."

I glanced at Holmes and I could see the mixed emotions on his face. While he was happy the cipher had been solved, I could tell that the idea of being bested by a machine nettled him.

Imp must have seen the reaction as well, for he said, "I'm certain you would have got it eventually, Holmes. The machine just saved you some time and labour."

"What does the message say?" asked Holmes.

"The message consisted of but two words, and while the machine has no idea what to do with them, I'm pretty certain you do."

"The words?"

"Cornwall and mount," replied Imp.

"Was there a key involved?"

"Obviously, otherwise I'm certain you would have solved it. The key was the Latin phrase *Deus vult*."

"*Deus vult*?" I exclaimed.

"'God wills it' was the battle cry of the crusaders," explained Holmes. Then turning to Imp, he said, "I tried that phrase."

"I'm certain you did," replied Imp.

"So why did it fail to work?"

"They added an extra layer of security which no one could have anticipated," explained Imp.

"An extra layer of security?" I asked

"It was quite simple actually, but it makes the code virtually impossible to solve unless you get very lucky or have an inordinate amount of time to devote to it."

"How did it work?" asked Holmes.

"They simply added a negative three to each letter. So your D had to count back three letters to become A, and your E becomes B and so on. It's quite involved as you can imagine."

"Why three?" I asked aloud.

Holmes said, "There are any number of possibilities. The three might have been a reference to what the Catholics call the Holy Trinity or it might refer to the Templar symbol of two knights sharing one horse. The ancient Greeks considered three the 'perfect' number for myriad reasons. The really clever part is making it a negative three rather a positive number. However, what's important is that we know the number – not necessarily why it was chosen – and as a result, we now know the message."

I must say that after he had said his piece, Holmes looked a little less pained, and he thanked Imp effusively. "If I can ever repay the favour," said Holmes, "all you have to do is ask."

We thanked Imp and left, and Holmes was a changed man on the way back to Baker Street. Finally, he was a step ahead of his adversaries, and I could almost see the wheels turning as he sought a way to make the most of that advantage.

When we had returned to our rooms, he said, "I'm going to ask Green to join us tonight and if possible to bring his linguist and historian. I'm going to request that he come at half seven and his companions arrive at eight. That will give me thirty minutes to bring him up to speed, and then he can decide what he wants to share with them although I'm going to suggest that all confidences be kept to a minimum."

He sat at the table, composed a brief note and summoned the boy in buttons to deliver it. "Please wait for a reply," Holmes stressed. He then handed the lad a few coins, "It will be much faster if you take a cab."

He then strode into his bedroom and emerged a few minutes later in his dressing gown. Picking up his violin, he began to play. I couldn't identify the piece and I'm inclined to think it was a composition he had created. At any rate, this was a totally different Holmes from the driven man who had laboured so mightily to break that deuced code just a few days ago.

We enjoyed a quiet dinner of roast lamb with potatoes and greens, and I was just pouring glasses of sherry when I heard the bell sound. "That would be Captain Green, I believe," said Holmes.

Sure enough, within a few minutes Green had entered the flat, settled into the chair indicated by Holmes, and joined us in the sherry. "Since you sent for me, I can only assume you have good news," Green said.

"Indeed," replied Holmes, "the code has been broken." He then proceeded to explain the key and the negative three, but he omitted all mention of the machine. I don't think he did it as a show of self-aggrandisement. Rather, I'm inclined to think he didn't want to upset Green by telling him that another outside party had been involved – even to a slight degree.

When he had finished, he looked at Green and said, "What, if anything, can you tell me about the Knights Templar and their holdings in Cornwall?"

"I know for certain they had a presence there. In fact, I believe there are at least two locations in Cornwall connected with the Templars; however, for the particulars I think you would be better served by consulting with the historian I've employed, Steven Smith. I've asked him and the linguist, her name is Joan Falcetta, to meet me here at eight as you requested." Pulling a handsome gold Hunter from his waistcoat pocket, he glanced at it and said they should be here in just a few minutes. "I know Steven places a premium on punctuality," he added.

It was perhaps two or three minutes later that the bell rang, and that was followed by the sounds of feet on the stairs. Our landlady knocked, and I said, "Come in, Mrs. Hudson."

She opened the door and said, "A Miss Falcetta and a Mr. Smith. They said they are expected."

"Indeed, they are, Mrs. Hudson, and if you would be so kind as send up another pot of coffee, it would be greatly appreciated."

She nodded with the patience of one long used to untimely requests from her tenants, and said, "Just give me a few minutes, Mr. Holmes." He thanked her and then turned to our guests whom I had seated at the dining room table.

Green took care of the introductions, and while he was doing so, I had the opportunity to take stock of our new acquaintances. Miss Falcetta, I was told, had attended classes at the University of Padua as well as the Sorbonne. She was small and petite with dark brown eyes and a fetching smile, yet she also exuded a certain scholarly seriousness.

By contrast, her companion, Robert Smith, the historian, was a tall man, taller than Holmes, with a pronounced burr that marked him as a native of Scotland. He had studied history at Edinburgh and then pursued additional courses at Cambridge.

Having allowed the introductions to conclude, Holmes then said, "What can either or both of you tell me about the Knights Templar and their locations in Cornwall?"

The two looked at Green and then at each other, and she nodded to Smith and said, "You go first, and I'll add anything I know when you have finished."

Smith cleared his throat and then began, "It is commonly believed there were two Templar sites in Cornwall. As you are aware, the Templars established churches and hostels for travelers and pilgrims throughout Europe. The Temple church they built in Cornwall in the middle of the Bodmin Moor, which was dedicated to St. Catherine, dates from the early 12th century and probably served as a haven for those traveling from the west of Britain and Ireland. They would cross the moors, thus avoiding the dangerous coastal waters, and then embark from harbours on the southwest coast for Santiago de Compostela, Rome and the Holy Land."

He paused and then asked, "Shall I touch on the legends about the Holy Grail and the Ark of the Covenant – both of which have Templar connections?"

"Since you refer to them as legends, I think we can safely dispense with the apocrypha," replied Holmes.

"You said there were two locations? What was the other?" I asked.

"The other, though far more interesting and certainly more scenic, has, at best, a tenuous connection to the Templars."

"You are talking about Mount St. Michael?" inquired Miss Falcetta.

"Indeed, I am," replied Smith. "In Mount's Bay right off the coast of the village of Marazion, there is a small tidal island known as Mount St. Michael. Although it's not terribly far from the coast, between three quarters of a mile and a mile, the only ways to reach it are on foot via a causeway or by boat. I should also mention the causeway is under water at high tide.

"It is generally believed that in the 11th century, Edward the Confessor gifted the island to the Benedictines. As you know Bernard of Clairveaux was a Benedictine and there is a sister monastery in France named Mont Saint-Michael," he said, emphasizing the difference in pronunciation. I must say hearing a Scotsman essay the French tongue with some success was quite unexpected.

He must have seen the look on my face, for he chuckled and said, "I'll admit it's not my first language, but I do the best I can." He then looked at Miss Falcetta, "Would you care to continue?"

She smiled, "The monastery in France is also on a tidal island, and they are quite similar in shape and size. Mont Saint-Michael," she said with a perfect Parisian accent, "was originally the abbey for its English counterpart. As Robert said, the connection of the English island to the Templars is not absolute, but for many historians the Benedictine link, and the fact that it is dedicated to St. Michael the warrior archangel have proven suggestive."

At that Smith said, "The island in Cornwall has a long history but not a great deal is known about the Templars there except what little we have told you."

"How far is it from the Temple Church on the moor to Mount St. Michael?" asked Holmes.

"I couldn't say with absolute certainty, but I would estimate it at about sixty miles," replied Smith.

That seemed to give Holmes food for thought, and he suddenly lapsed into silence.

After a few minutes, when no one said anything, it became uncomfortable, so I attempted to lighten the mood. Turning to Smith, I asked, "Are there any legends about the island?"

Smith replied, "Would you believe me if I said some people have traced the origin of the Jack the Giant-Killer and thus the Jack and the Beanstalk tales to it?" I couldn't tell whether he was pulling my leg or speaking seriously, but I made a mental note to research that particular fact at some point in the future.

At that moment Mrs. Hudson arrived with coffee and slices of a chocolate cake that she had baked earlier in the day, and we sat about the table discussing the events of the day.

Finally, Smith asked, "I don't suppose you'd care to tell us what this is all about?"

Suddenly all eyes were on Holmes, "I do not mean this in an unkind way, but in this instance, I believe that the less you know the safer you will be."

I could see disappointment flash across both his and Miss Falcetta's faces, but I think they understood the gravity of the situation. Holmes then added, "I appreciate your patience and understanding, and I promise when this is over that you will be made privy to all."

That seemed to mollify them to a degree, and the mood in the room once again lightened. Perhaps forty minutes later, Smith and Miss Falcetta departed, and then Green looked at Holmes expectantly and asked, "So what do we do now?"

Holmes said, "Now that we have a destination and two possible sites, I want to give it some thought and do a bit more research. Shall we meet for dinner tomorrow? I'll reserve a private table at Simpson's. Say seven o'clock?"

"That would be splendid," replied Green."

"We will see you then," replied Holmes. Then he cautioned Green, "You are now in possession of some very valuable information. You will take care?"

Patting the pocket of his coat, he smiled and said, "I will but believe me, I can handle myself."

Chapter 12

Although I awoke earlier than usual the next morning in anticipation of our meeting with Lestrade, I was not surprised to find Holmes sitting at the breakfast table reading the papers and enjoying a cup of coffee. I poured one for myself and rang the bell for breakfast. A few minutes later, Mrs. Hudson appeared with a tray laden with scrambled eggs, rashers of bacon, toast and kippers. Looking at me, she smiled and said, "Make sure you leave a good amount for Inspector Lestrade."

I was just tucking into my eggs when the bell sounded. "That would be Lestrade, punctual as ever," said Holmes. I looked at the clock on the mantel and saw that it was exactly eight.

A moment later Lestrade had joined us. "Enjoy your breakfast," Holmes said, "then you can tell us what you've learned about the Knights Templar."

Lestrade took Holmes at his word and loaded his plate. Some fifteen minutes later, he popped the last piece of bacon in his mouth, finished his coffee and sat back contentedly. "I began by examining some of the secret societies that exist in London today – the Freemasons, the Rosicrucians and the Golden Dawn. As you know most operate quite openly; what makes them 'secret' are their initiation rites, their special handshakes and other such rituals which are known only to members.

"Initially, I turned up nothing, so I decided to adopt a different approach. I told a co-worker I was interested in joining the Rosicrucians, and could he tell me a bit about the group."

"I should have thought you'd begin with the Masons," I offered. "After all, they date back to the Middle Ages as do the Templars."

Lestrade cast a baleful look at me, and for just a second I was reminded of Holmes, and then the inspector said, "As you well know, Doctor, Pope Leo XIII has spoken out against the Masons on more than one occasion. I didn't think a group decried by the Holy See would have anything to do with the legendary warrior monks."

"And you were right to think so," interjected Holmes. "By the way, Watson, I should like to point out the Rosicrucians have as their symbol a rosy cross. Sound familiar? Pray continue, Inspector."

Lestrade gave us another glance, but he continued, "This Rosicrucians were officially established in Germany in the mid-17th century. While some claim it was founded in the mid-14th century, there are others who maintain that the group can trace its origins to the mysteries of ancient Egypt. I shall leave that for you to decide.

"At any rate, the history of the group is uncertain. Some say it was founded by a Christian Rosenkreuz while others claim that he was an entirely fictitious figure. I'm not inclined to see much of a link to the Templars there, but then again I'm no expert," he said, glancing at Holmes.

"Then, of course," he continued, "there are the various chivalric orders such as the Order of the Bath, the Order of the Thistle and the Order of the Garter. I didn't have time to dig as deeply as I would have liked, so anything you can add to my suggestions would be greatly appreciated," and with that Lestrade concluded his report and poured himself another cup of coffee."

"And you have heard nothing of the Templars?" I asked.

"The little bits that I came across were nothing more than whispers, and whispers aren't rumours – let alone facts. It was so vague, it hardly seemed worth mentioning.

"I mean everyone knows the Templars are connected to the Inner Temple. Well that's about as far as I got."

"All things considered, you have done well in such a limited amount of time, but the group we are seeking – if indeed it is a group, and if there are whispers, I'm inclined to think there is – operates in the shadows. It would be a small, tight-knit cohort of men with a common background and a belief in the old ways. If I am correct, they would all be Catholic, and they might hail from some of the Empire's oldest families."

"You can't be serious," I exclaimed.

"What else can we conclude? They are seeking the Templar treasure, they are familiar with the history of the organization, they employ the same titles used by that group and they know and use the code; fortunately, they don't know how to break this version of it – yet."

"So what will you do, Holmes?" Lestrade asked.

"If there is such a group, I know of one person who would be aware of its existence, and I know exactly where to find him – in the bow window of his St. James's Street club."

"Really, Holmes? You believe him reliable?"

"In a matter such as this – I would consider him above reproach." With that he donned his coat and hat, bid Lestrade and me good morning and stalked out the door.

Lestrade looked at me questioningly.

"He's off to see an old friend of his from university," I explained, "who now makes his living as an ink-stained wretch for some of the garbage papers that cater to inquisitive minds."

Lestrade just remarked, "I suppose he knows all sorts of odd people." With that he finished his coffee and bade me good day. As he reached the door, he turned and said, "Please thank Mrs. Hudson for the breakfast and tell Mr. Holmes I'll be in touch if I discover anything else. You might also inform him that a degree of reciprocity would be appreciated."

With the morning to myself, I decided to head to the British Library and see if I could discover anything. When I arrived, I explained to the librarian, whom I knew by sight, that I was researching the Crusades for a novel I was considering.

"But you won't stop writing stories about Mr. Holmes?" he inquired with a hint of urgency in his voice.

After I promised that I would continue recording Holmes's exploits, he led me to a small room and twenty minutes later, I had no fewer than thirty volumes about the Crusades in front of me.

"Many of these are in French and a few are in Latin and German," he explained. "I wasn't certain if you spoke or read the languages, but I figured I'd bring them along."

I was stunned to see books by Hume and Voltaire as well as by Thomas Fuller and Gibbon. I had no idea the Templars had aroused such interest over the centuries. Feeling totally overwhelmed, I scanned the few books in English in a rather haphazard fashion, but I soon realized this was a task best left to the professionals. Besides, I told myself, any secrets they knew, they probably kept to themselves.

Feeling dispirited, I gave up after nearly three hours. On my way out I thanked the librarian profusely and said I'd found exactly what I'd expected. I also had to reassure him once again that I would continue to chronicle Holmes's adventures. Although I am not normally a fan of prevarication, in this instance, I rationalized my little white lie by thinking the man would feel that he had served me well. My shortcomings as a researcher should cast no reflections on him.

I arrived home to an empty flat and wondered how Holmes might be faring in his endeavours. Around six. I heard his tread on the stairs, and a moment later he entered the flat. It was impossible to read the expression on his face, so I remained silent, knowing he would tell me the results of his labours when he was ready and not a moment before.

He entered his bedroom and emerged a few minutes later in his blue dressing gown. After charging his pipe and lighting it with a vesta, he finally looked at me and said, "Did your visit to the library prove fruitful? Researching the Crusades can be a decidedly dull affair – especially for a neophyte."

"Holmes, are you having me followed?"

He chuckled and said, "Not at all, my friend. How often have I told you that you see but you do not observe?"

"More times than I care to remember?"

"Well, had you observed those around you at the library, you might have noticed me sitting at a table over to the side."

"Well, if you saw me why didn't you say hello."

"I was about to but when I heard you promising the librarian that you would keep up your Boswellian duties, I decided silence was preferable to the idle chatter I knew would ensue."

"He is a great admirer of yours, Holmes."

"Which is precisely why I decided to continue my research uninterrupted."

"And what exactly did your research entail? When you left this morning, I thought you were going to see Langdale Pike."

"I did, and while he believes such a group exists, like friend Lestrade, he has no solid proof. I must say, I was rather disappointed in his reply. Despite his reputation, he always manages to stay *au courant* with such matters. As he says, you never know what bit of information may come in handy."

"So what brought you to the library?"

"I was attempting to learn as much as I could about the topography of the two Templar holdings in Cornwall. As you know they are quite different. So before I continue, let me pose a question to you: If you were a Templar charged with hiding a treasure of some value, where would you conceal it?

"Your choices, as you know, are a small tidal island or a church built near a small village."

"I should think the answer is obvious," I replied. "I should choose the island as I think defending it from any hostile invaders would be much easier. Conquerors would have to come by boat which certainly puts them in a perilous position. Archers with longbows, which were first used by the Welsh against the English more than a century earlier, could fire at the boats as they approached. Although the island is not large, the treasure could be hidden anywhere – even in the sea."

"You certainly make a compelling case, but I think I have to side with the church for all the reasons you have cited. There is also one serious drawback to storing the treasure on an island."

"Oh?"

"Yes, you are cut off from all supplies, including possibly fresh water. Moreover, you have no way of communicating with the mainland."

"I must admit I hadn't considered that aspect."

"We know the Temple Church has a definite link to the Templars, having been built in 1120 on land owned by the Knights. After the Templars were disbanded, the church passed to the Knights Hospitallers, also known as the Order of St John. It eventually achieved a degree of notoriety as a place where marriages could be performed without banns or licenses – similar to Gretna Green in Scotland – but that practice ended more than a century ago.

"With no real congregation and benefactors to speak of, the church was allowed to decay and fall into ruin, and by the middle of this century, the building was in a terrible state of disrepair. A final service was held on the 29th of January 1882, in front of a "large congregation," and then the church was rebuilt the following year.

"It lacks all modern conveniences and there are few people around. I believe services are held infrequently. In short, it was never a very busy place, but the rebuilding may complicate our task to some degree."

"Why do you say that?"

"Because any clues that may have been hidden in the architecture, any code markings that may have provided a hint have probably been lost."

"So you are saying that we have a formidable task in front of us?"

"You also have a grand gift for understatement, old friend. Still, those victories that are hard fought are most relished."

"So what's to be done?"

"I believe a trip to Cornwall is in order."

"Will you ask Green to accompany us?"

"I don't see how we can leave him behind, besides his expertise may prove invaluable. Perhaps he can bring some of the knowledge he gleaned on his Jerusalem expeditions to bear on a humble country church in Cornwall."

"Or a tidal island?" I ventured.

"Still sticking to your theory, Watson?"

"For the moment. I'm certain there are flaws to your selection as well."

"Indeed there are, but they pale when compared to those one might endure trying to survive a siege at Mount St. Michael."

Pausing to consider everything Holmes had just said, I then asked, "And what about Lestrade? Will you continue to keep the official force at bay?"

"I think for the present that seems the best course to follow. I will inform Lestrade of our destination and suggest he keep himself available should the need arise. I will also see if he knows any of the local constabulary although given the remoteness of the Temple Church, I am not optimistic."

Although I had a few reservations, I couldn't find any great fault with his logic and decided to keep my concerns to myself for the most part. However, I did feel compelled to voice at least one objection which I had developed: "Holmes, what if they divided the treasure, concealing a portion at the Temple Church and the remainder on the island?"

Holmes turned around, looked at me and then exclaimed, "Bravo, Watson! You make an excellent point. So I suppose that we had better prepare for a rather prolonged stay in Cornwall. If the search at the Temple Church proves fruitless, we will move on to Mount St. Michael. And now it appears we must travel south even if we are successful at the first location."

I must have been beaming with pride, and I found it hard to believe that I had tumbled to something so obvious that had escaped my flat mate's attention. However, I was soon brought back to reality when Holmes continued, "Of course that just begs that question of what our course of action must be if searches at both places come a cropper."

"Can't we then conclude there is no treasure to be found?"

"I think not. Have you forgot our nocturnal encounter with those brigands in the park and the theft at the Wallace Collection? I am fairly certain, as is Green, there is a Templar treasure of some sort hidden somewhere; it just remains to us to make certain that we find it before they do."

"And what will you do with this treasure when you find it?" I asked, making certain to use *when* not *if.*

"I would think that is largely Captain Green's decision although I would expect the bulk, if not all, of it to end up in museums around the country."

"Do you think the Crown might try to claim it under the guise that it should have been King Edward's when the Templars were dissolved?"

"While I can certainly envision other monarchs putting forth such a claim, I find it difficult to imagine Her Majesty doing so. That being said, one can never predict the exigencies of government."

"Yes, I suppose it would reflect rather poorly on the Queen. Still, there are any number of ministers with which she has to contend."

"Happily, that is one problem with which we need not concern ourselves. Now let us enjoy what Mrs. Hudson has prepared for dinner, and then we can make plans for our trip to Cornwall."

Upon hearing his words, I must admit that my pulse raced a bit. My existence had become rather humdrum these past few months, and I found I was looking forward to sharing yet another adventure with Holmes. As he was wont to say on more than one occasion, "The game is afoot!"

Chapter 13

I came down to breakfast the next morning to discover that Holmes once again had eaten and departed. "He was up before seven o'clock," Mrs. Hudson informed me. "He gave me this note to give the page when he arrives, and he told me to tell you that you might want to start packing."

When Mrs. Hudson showed me the note, I could see that it was addressed to Green, and I wondered if he were being given the same instructions as I. At any rate, after finishing my breakfast, I went to Barts where, during my rounds I informed my superior I was going out of town for a few days, possibly longer. Fortunately, things were slow, and I knew I wouldn't be missed there.

When I returned late in the afternoon, Holmes was sitting at his chemistry table working on an experiment of some sort. When I entered, he placed the test tube in a rack, extinguished the Bunsen burner, and turned to me, "I assume Mrs. Hudson passed my instructions along to you. I should have realized you had to attend to your duties at the hospital. At any rate, I'd suggest that you pack after dinner. I plan to leave tonight."

"Tonight? Have you even heard from Captain Green?"

"Yes, he will be accompanying us. I have arranged for a hansom to be outside at midnight. We will then pick up Green, head to Paddington, and depart from there at one."

"One o'clock? I thought you said you wanted to leave tonight."

"I did and I do."

"You mean one in the morning?"

"Obviously."

"But why?"

"Because we are still being watched, but I have discerned their schedule. For the past few days, their sentries have been leaving at eleven and not returning until six a.m."

"You can't be serious!" I exclaimed as I headed towards the window to see if I could locate the watcher.

Holmes stopped me, "Don't look, Watson. I think by ignoring them these last few days and making no secret of our moves, I have lulled them into a false sense of security."

"Are they following both of us?"

"They were, but yesterday, there was only one person watching, and he tailed me. That's why I say they have become complacent.

"If we can slip away tonight, we may well be in Cornwall before they even realize their mistake. Plus, to add to the illusion, I've arranged for Lestrade to stop here at various times throughout the day and evening in our absence. The good inspector was only too willing to help when he learned that breakfast and dinner would be included."

I wondered if Lestrade realized how fortunate he was. One of my chief complaints about my adventures with Holmes had always been that our meals were irregular in the extreme, and the food was often average at best – and sometimes a good deal worse. Still, that was a small price to pay for the privilege of supporting my friend.

As if he were reading my mind, Holmes remarked, "I'm told that the fare in Cornwall can be quite delicious – especially the pasties and the pilchards."

I smiled to myself and wondered once again how he was able to divine my thoughts so easily.

In honor of our departure, Mrs. Hudson had prepared a delicious meal of roasted chicken with potatoes and runner beans. She had also baked scones which she served with clotted cream and jam for dessert. "I don't know where you're going," she remarked, "but at least you can't say I didn't send you off with full stomachs. I'll pack a few scones for the trip as well," she said glancing at me.

"That's not necessary," said Holmes.

"They're not for you," she replied tartly.

I thanked her profusely and she departed. After a cigar and a glass of port, I headed to my room to pack and perhaps take a short nap. As I ascended the stairs, Holmes said, "Watson, do remember to pack your sidearm. One can never be too careful. I'll wake you at half eleven."

As an old campaigner, I packed quickly and efficiently. After cleaning and oiling my pistol, I considered placing it in my bag and then decided to keep it in my coat pocket. "You never know when you may need it," I told myself.

I rested for the next few hours, occasionally dozing off for a few minutes, but I was wide awake when Holmes tapped on my door at half eleven. After making some last-minute preparations, checking to make certain the sentries had left and penning a note to Lestrade, we donned our coats, descended the stairs and opened the front door to find a growler waiting for us at the kerb. Holmes spoke to the driver, and we started off in the direction of Mayfair. Perhaps ten minutes later, we stopped at a house on Maddux Street on the other side of Grosvenor Square.

Green, who had been standing outside waiting, climbed in and greeted us. At that point, I wondered whether Green knew we were still being followed, but I kept the thought to myself and made a note to ask Holmes about it later.

After pleasantries had been exchanged and Holmes had given the driver his instructions, Green began by saying "I didn't think trains ran so late at night."

"Normally, they don't," replied Holmes, "but we are taking a special. I have a friend who works in the government and he has arranged everything."

At that point I was certain that Holmes had involved his brother, Mycroft. Once again I held my tongue, and when I glanced at Holmes in the near darkness of the cab, he merely looked at me and gave a slight nod of the head as if to confirm my suspicion.

The streets were virtually empty, and there was but one other cab on Westminster Bridge. As we crossed over the span, our horses' hooves the only noise in the otherwise still night, I heard Big Ben sound the quarter hour and thought that we were making excellent time. The cabbie drove to the far side of the station, and we stepped down; I checked my watch and noted that it was 12:50. Although there were no trains arriving or departing, the station was not entirely empty. There were a few men pushing brooms about the station and the various platforms, and I spotted a few others sleeping on benches. I assumed they had missed the last train and were stuck here until morning.

We made our way to a small sidetrack where a train consisting of a locomotive, a passenger car and what appeared to be a mail car was waiting for us. The engine was belching steam and there was but a single guard on duty.

He approached my friend and said, "Mr. Holmes, it was requested that I deliver this to you personally."

Holmes took the large envelope, opened it and withdrew a single sheet of paper. After he had read it, he folded it and thrust it back into the envelope which he placed in the Gladstone he was carrying. "Thank you for that," he said, "and please express my gratitude to the colleagues in your department."

We then boarded the train, and a few minutes later, under cover of a dreary London sky, we were on our way to Plymouth.

As you might expect, I was anxious to know what was in the envelope, but I waited, knowing Holmes would share that information when he was ready. Green, however, was not nearly so reticent. After we had pulled out of the station, he looked at Holmes and asked, "Did that envelope you received have anything to do with our journey?"

"As a matter of fact, it did," Holmes replied. Pulling the envelope from his Gladstone, he opened it and extracted several papers. "My friend in the government," he said without elaborating further, "arranged this train. Normally, it's just a mail train, hence the extra car. Under ordinary circumstances, it departs at six each morning for Plymouth. Fortunately, he was able to alter the schedule, and he also provided me with some up-to-date maps of the areas in question as well."

"Excellent," replied Green. "So at least we are not going in totally blind."

Holmes smiled, "That's a situation I strive to avoid at all costs. Now might I suggest that you and Dr. Watson try to sleep? I expect that we will have rather a long day in front of us."

While Holmes continued poring over his maps, Green and I and stretched out on seats that were designed to hold two or three passengers. I bundled my coat under my head for a pillow and from where I was resting I could see Holmes's hawk-like face studying the maps in search of even the tiniest bit of information that might help us in this rather daunting quest.

I have no idea how long I slept, but I was awakened on at least two occasions when we stopped. The third time this happened, I saw that Holmes was now sitting back, smoking his pipe and gazing out into the night. Glancing at Green, I realized he was still asleep, so I rose quietly and went to sit with my friend.

Before I could speak, he began, "This is certainly one of the most singular cases that has ever come our way, is it not, old friend?"

"I won't argue the point."

"And yet I wouldn't have missed it for the world. We have gone from some tallow droppings in a museum to an attempt to locate a medieval treasure that may prove priceless – or may not even exist any longer."

"I certainly hope it's the former. Although I am willing to make certain sacrifices for Queen and Country, pretending to sleep on that bench in the park doesn't number among them."

Holmes chuckled, and then turning serious, he said, "We should be pulling into Plymouth soon. From there we must take another train to Bodmin, which is about seven miles from the Temple Church. We can either stay in Bodmin or take rooms at the Old Inn in St. Breward, which is located on the western side of Bodmin Moor, perhaps five miles from the church."

"Certainly, closer would be better," I offered.

"If geography were our only consideration, I would, of course, agree with you. However, the more remote we are, the more removed we are."

"Removed?"

"From the local constabulary, from shops, and, perhaps most importantly; from people who might be of assistance should the need arise. While staying in Bodmin has its obvious advantages, I think you may be correct and we must weigh those against proximity to the church."

"Don't forget to include the extra time spent traveling to and from Bodmin every day. Think it over, Holmes. You know I will abide by your decision."

"Good old Watson. You do remain a fixed point in an ever-changing universe."

He then lapsed into silence, and perhaps twenty minutes later, we pulled into Plymouth. The screaming of the brakes awoke Green, and after we had boarded the local train and taken our seats, I discovered we were fortunate in that initially we were the only passengers on board. Holmes then went over the lodging possibilities, and Green said, "I think the Old Inn might serve us better. The monks used to stay at the inn – of course, it wasn't an inn then – when they were building the parish church which was dedicated to St. Branwalader or St. Breward although that is some distance away.

"I know you don't believe in legends, Mr. Holmes, but there are any number of places in the vicinity of Bodmin Moor which are associated with the King Arthur."

"Do tell," I said.

Green looked at Holmes, "If I may?"

Holmes gave a dismissive gesture and Green returned his gaze to me and began, "Not too far from the Temple Church, certainly fewer than ten miles and less as the crow flies – is Drozmary Pool. Many who believe in the legend of King Arthur hold that this pool was the dwelling place of Viviane or Nimue, the Lady of the Lake, the woman who gave Arthur his sword, Excalibur.

"Another point of interest for believers is Tintagel Castle, which is located on the coast and generally regarded as Arthur's birthplace. It's quite an interesting site, with half the castle having been constructed on the mainland and the other half on the headland."

Holmes merely snorted.

Glancing at Holmes, I could see the disinterest on his face, and I knew that when he was working on a problem, he hated to be distracted. At that point I determined to end the discussion of King Arthur and get back to the matter at hand even though I found Green's tales fascinating. As diplomatically as possible, I said, "Certainly when this is all over, I should like to visit there, but I think we're going to have our hands full for the foreseeable future."

"Quite right," said Green, who then lapsed into a silence that matched Holmes's own.

The train chugged along and after a few stops we arrived in the town of Bodmin. Holmes asked one of the porters where the closest stable might be found. He was given directions, and after a short walk through the rather quaint streets, we arrived at O'Leary's Stables. Holmes inquired about leasing a carriage for a week or two, but the owner told us that he had recently rented his last available wagon.

"Where is it that you want to go?" he asked.

"We are hoping to spend a few days at the Old Inn," Holmes replied. "Do you think, they'll have rooms available?"

"Maggie always finds room for paying customers," he laughed. "If you'd like I'll drive you there in my cart."

"Is there a stable near the inn?" I asked.

"There is, but if John O'Keefe has nothing to rent, I can talk to my son-in-law who lives about a mile from the inn. I can also check in Millpool which is on the way and see if my friend, Roger, is using his cart."

"Should we have something to eat here?" I asked. "With everything at sixes and sevens who knows when we may get another chance to eat?"

Although Holmes was eager to be on our way, Green seconded my motion, and O'Leary sent us along to Elizabeth Rowe, who ran the inn in town. She was only too happy to have three for breakfast. Some twenty minutes later we were enjoying a full Cornish breakfast which included eggs, bacon and sausages, fried bread and beans, mushrooms and tomato, fried potato and Hog's Pudding, a Cornish specialty. When she found out we were heading to the Old Inn, she sniffed, "The food there is edible, I suppose, but I'll pack you a basket if you like – just in case."

And so it was that nearly an hour later, we returned to O'Leary's who had hitched two draft horses to his cart. Holmes sat on the seat with O'Leary while Green and I clambered into the back along with our bags.

As we rode along, O'Leary asked, "What brings you gentlemen to this part of the country?"

"We plan to explore some of the old ruins on the moor," Holmes said.

"Well, there's no shortage of those," he laughed. "Depending upon how long you are here, you'll want to make certain you see the Hurlers, Rillaton Barrow, the Trippet Stones and Leskernick. Along the way, you'll no doubt encounter a passel of other monuments, including all types of menhirs and cairns."

Green was obviously intrigued and asked, "Which is your favorite?"

"I'm partial to the Hurlers, myself, but they are all interesting."

Perhaps an hour later, we arrived at Millpool, a charming hamlet located right on the edge of Bodmin Moor. O'Leary inquired about a cart, but discovered that none was available. "I suppose I'll have to take you the rest of the way then."

As we drove along the moor, I was taken aback by the unspoiled beauty of this natural wonderland. It also recalled the days I had spent in Baskerville Hall near Dartmoor as Holmes tried to solve the mystery of the hound. The land was rough with high tors here and there, and occasionally we could see the stone piles that our distant ancestors had once considered home. Under other circumstances, it might have seemed bleak or even forbidding, but under a bright June sky, there was nothing fearsome about the landscape.

After perhaps forty minutes, Green suddenly broke the silence, asking, "How far are we from the Temple Church?"

O'Leary replied, "It's over that way a bit, perhaps a mile or so. I can stop there now if you like."

Holmes shot Green a reproving glance and then said smoothly, "We'll have plenty of time to take a look at that. I'm certain there are some ruins nearby that we'll be inspecting."

"'Deed there are," laughed O'Leary, who then continued, "If you'd come about twenty years ago, you could have explored the church itself. Although it had been allowed to fall into disrepair, it was rebuilt back in the early '80s."

"Interesting," said Green, "does any of the old church remain?"

"Nowt that I know of," laughed O'Leary, "but I'm told some of the original stones and crosses can be seen as they were used to construct a small outbuilding."

Holmes then cast a withering look at Green who immediately lapsed into silence.

"Not too much longer now," O'Leary offered. "Off to your right, you have the Trippet Stone Circle. We've had our share of folks up here to look at them. And then less than a mile away you can find the Stripple stones. If you go there, be careful. The stones are surrounded by a small ditch, so you'll want to go on a dry day or risk losing a shoe in the mud."

Holmes then began to pepper O'Leary with questions about the stones in both locations. Obviously something had piqued his interest or he was deliberately trying to focus the driver's attention on the stone circles rather than the church. Unfortunately O'Leary didn't know enough to answer many of Holmes inquiries. "Perhaps, Mr. Broad the owner of the Old Inn will be able to help you – he's lived here his whole life, having inherited the inn from his father."

Holmes then sat there cradling his chin in his hand, and I was familiar with that pose. I knew he was pondering something of significance. I just couldn't tell with any degree of certainty what it was.

146

Thirty minutes later, we finally arrived at the Old Inn. Standing in front of the inn was the landlord, Mr. John Broad, who had come out to greet us. He was a mountain of a man, who lived up to his name. Perhaps in his mid-forties, he had a thick mane of dark hair with luxurious side-whiskers that gave him a rather severe air. However, he greeted us warmly and said he had plenty of rooms to let as a party had departed only the day before. More important, he had a cart and two horses that he could put at our disposal – for a small daily fee, which he could reduce if we took it for the week.

"What brings you gentlemen to this god-forsaken place?" he asked in a thick Cornish accent.

"Captain Green is an antiquarian. He is interested in the menhirs and henges that can be found in this area," explained Holmes smoothly. "Dr. Watson and I are his colleagues. However, he is the professional while we are mere amateurs."

"I suppose you've seen Stonehenge?" asked Broad of Green.

"Many times," replied the captain.

"Well, we have nothing here nearly as grand as that, but I'm told that scientists find them interesting nonetheless."

O'Leary, who had carried our bags into the inn, emerged at that point. "Stay for supper, Danny?" asked Broad.

"I'd like to but I'd best be getting back." Having said that, he stood there stolidly. As Holmes and Green had already entered the inn, it then struck me that I had been left to pay the man. I settled up and included a generous gratuity.

As he mounted his cart, he thanked me again and said, "If you return to Bodmin, stop by and I'll treat you to a pint, Doctor."

I joined Holmes and Green at the front desk, and after signing the register, we adjourned to the dining room for a late lunch. When I asked what was good, Mr. Broad smiled and said, "Everything! My wife is a great cook, but I'm partial to the Moorland Grill."

When I asked what was in it, he replied, "You'll get a nice piece of Cornish rump steak, chicken breast, pork sausage, gammon, a pork loin chop, a fried egg, mushrooms, onions, peas and grilled tomato."

"My word," I exclaimed, "that could feed the three of us for several days."

He laughed and said, "I'll have her make up a platter with extra eggs and you gents can sort it out amongst yourselves."

While we were waiting, I ordered three tankards of his best ale. "I have but one ale, but it's a pretty fair pint if I say so myself."

An hour later, we had devoured most of the platter, and I noticed that even Holmes ate with a hearty appetite, which I must admit I found surprising. After the meal, we went for a walk on the moor. Once we were out of sight of the tiny hamlet, it was as though we were in a foreign land. There were tors in the distance, and the vegetation, such as it is, was sparse and windblown, and once again I was reminded of my days in Dartmoor. I am sure similar thoughts had crossed Holmes's mind as well.

"Tomorrow, we will visit the church and see what we can learn from what remains of the original building. The recent reconstruction works against us," he observed, "but we won't know for certain until we examine it ourselves."

"And should we not find anything?" asked Green.

"Then we must journey south to Mount St. Michael and hope that we fare better there."

The thought that we would be unsuccessful was an unpleasant prospect, so I quickly changed the subject. "Before we leave, I should like to see those stone circles O'Leary told us about."

"Perhaps," replied Holmes cautiously, "first, let us attend to the business at hand and see how we fare tomorrow."

By now, we had returned to the inn, and as we entered, Mr. Broad came towards us and said, "This letter arrived for you shortly after you left for your constitutional. It was delivered by a messenger on horseback."

He then handed Holmes an envelope. "Where did the messenger come from?' asked Holmes.

"He was from Altarnun, a village a bit to the north and east of us."

Holmes thanked our host and we retired to our rooms. He nodded at me as he entered his room, and after a few minutes, I heard a soft knock on my door."

When he came in, I couldn't contain my curiosity and said, "Is it a letter from Mycroft? What does he say?"

"No, it's not from Mycroft. It's from our adversaries, for lack of a better term."

"My word! They know where we are? How did they find us?"

"I cannot answer that quite yet," replied Holmes. "although I have my suspicions. As for the contents…" he handed me a slip of paper, on which had been written two lines:

Last chance!

We will be in touch!

Chapter 14

"Have they cracked the code?" I asked.

"I should think the answer is obvious," replied Holmes. "They have either followed us here or anticipated our arrival."

"Well, they should be easy to locate," I offered. "After all, they are strangers, and this is a rather sparsely populated area."

"They could be anywhere," replied Holmes. "There are no fewer than fifteen villages or hamlets on the moor itself. They might even be sleeping rough or hiding in a barrow, either of which would make them virtually impossible to find."

"How did they break the code? You don't think they also used Babbage's machine, do you?"

"I'm inclined to doubt it, but there are other visionaries who have devised similar machines. Among them is Alfred Smee, who serves as Surgeon to the Bank of England. He and Babbage were certainly acquainted. Another possibility might be those who followed in the footsteps of Ada Byron, Lady Lovelace."

"Any relation to the poet?" I asked hoping to lighten the mood.

"As a matter of fact, she was his daughter, and while she shared his passion for poetry, she was also a gifted mathematician."

Needless to say, I was taken aback at this bit of news.

Unperturbed, Holmes continued, "Like Smee, she knew Babbage quite well; in fact, at one time she worked as an assistant to Babbage. As you might expect, they frequently exchanged letters. After an Italian wrote an article about Babbage's Analytical Engine, she was asked to translate it into English. As she did, she added her own notes which ended up being three times as long as the original. As a result of that publication, she ascended to the Olympus of pure mathematicians.

"In addition to Babbage, she moved in a circle that included most of the other leading figures of her day, among them Sir David Brewster, Charles Wheatstone, Charles Dickens and Michael Faraday."

"Might our adversaries have sought her help in cracking the cipher?"

"No, that would be impossible. Like her father, she died quite young, back in 1852. I believe she was but 36 at the time of her death." Then suddenly changing tack, he remarked, "How they solved the code is irrelevant. The important thing is that they are in the vicinity. Whether they know more or less than we do, remains to be seen. Although given the letter, I'm inclined to think we know more than they do; otherwise, why offer us another chance."

"So what's the plan?"

"We go about our business – but always keeping a watchful eye on our surroundings. The saving grace of this moor is that while there are places where one may find concealment, there's very little cover, rendering a sneak attack almost impossible."

"Well, I have my pistol if it should come to that and unless Green has changed his habits, he too is armed."

"Excellent! Tomorrow, we'll rent Broad's cart and make our way to the Temple Church. I have no idea what clues, if any, we may find, but it is a starting point."

The next morning, after fortifying ourselves with a hearty Cornish breakfast, we set out in the rented cart for Temple Church. Holmes and Green sat up front while I rode in the rear. It was close to two hours later when we arrived in the hamlet of Temple and made our way to the Temple Church, which was more properly named the Church of St. Catherine of Alexandria.

"I thought it was a Templar Church?" I offered.

"It is, but the Knights dedicated their churches to various saints they admired. St. Catherine was a fourth-century martyr, who after being tortured, was ordered beheaded by the Emperor Maxentius," explained Green.

There was no one around, so Holmes parked the cart in front of the church and headed for the outbuildings. On one of them, we could clearly see a few pieces of decorated stonework that seemed much older and far more worn than the rest of the building. Holmes examined each carefully with his lens and then said, "These tell me nothing. Perhaps if there were more fragments, we might have been able to piece something together although I am rather doubtful about that as well."

Pointing to one stone, Green said, "What do you make of this? Doesn't that resemble one or two of the letters from the Templar code?"

"Indeed, it does," replied Holmes. "I would say that the one on the left might be a 'D' while its companion is most assuredly an 'E.'"

Looking at the wall closely, I saw the two symbols – >▷ – badly worn and nearly covered with moss.

Holmes continued, "Of course, that would only hold true if the code were being used without a key or other device to conceal the true meaning of the letters. Still it appears to be the beginning of *deus* or god in Latin, which certainly seems appropriate. Unfortunately, as you just pointed out, Captain, there are but two letters and their presence really doesn't offer much of a clue."

"Perhaps there is something in the church itself that may provide us with a clue," I suggested.

We made our way to the church, which was a cozy one-storey building with a two-storey tower to one side. As there was no one to let us in, Holmes proceeded to pick the lock. We closed the door behind us and stood in a small church, perhaps twenty feet wide and forty long.

Green remarked, "What makes this unusual among Templar churches is that it was not built in the shape of a circle."

Ignoring us, Holmes began to inspect the floor and the altar. During my own explorations, I discovered a depiction of a knight on horseback in what I later learned was the north window. I summoned Holmes and Green, and after examining it, Holmes said, "I can see no clues there."

"Well, there is also the cross in the stained-glass window on the east side," added Green.

"I've been looking at that and wondering if in some way it might provide an indication of any kind."

"How so?" I asked.

"That is what I am trying to ascertain," said Holmes with a grin. "Would you happen to know the feast day of St. Catherine of Alexandria?" asked Holmes of Green.

"I am pretty certain that it is the 25th of November," replied Green.

"Were there any other days that might have been significant to the Templars who built this church?" asked Holmes.

"There are many. I'm sure they regarded the 18th of January – the day deMolay was burned at the stake – as holy. In 1099 on the 13th of June, Jerusalem fell to an army of Crusaders. The 13th of October is often regarded as Templar Remembrance Day because that was the day King Philip ordered the arrests of all the members of the order in France. The 14th of November is also important because it begins the season of Lent."

"I was under the impression Christians celebrated Lent in the spring – before Easter?" I ventured.

"As a rule, they do," replied Green, "but the Templars celebrated two Lents every year – one before Easter and one before Christmas."

"Interesting as those facts may be, none of them appears to advance our investigation," remarked Holmes. "I think it is safe to assume that if the treasure were stored here or if even half the treasure were hidden here and the remainder moved elsewhere, there would be some kind of clue as to its location. The problem is the recent reconstruction appears to have muddied things beyond all recognition.

"Aside from the outbuilding is there anything here that remains of the original?" Holmes asked Green.

"I'm not certain. I do know the reconstruction was carried out by the Cornish architect Silvanus Trevail. I also know that during the reconstruction an old ash tree which had sprung up within the ruined walls had to be removed. When the workers cut the tree down and removed the stump, they discovered a human skeleton entwined within the roots."

"What became of the bones?" asked Holmes with just a tinge of excitement in his voice.

"There is no record of what Trevail did with the bones or where he had them buried," replied Green.

"Anything else?" asked Holmes with just a hint of frustration creeping into his voice.

"I believe Trevail used as many of the stones from the original floor as possible. I also understand that the stained-glass windows – although not original except for a few random pieces here and there – are exact copies of the designs from the originals. Apparently, someone had sketched them and presented the drawings to Trevail when the reconstruction began."

Holmes looked at the east window, with its depiction of the Templar cross. He then turned his attention to the other windows – one of which depicted St. Catherine, another of which depicted St. Francis of Assisi. Finally he turned his attention to three windows directly above the altar.

"Of course," he said to himself, as he appeared to focus on the top window.

Below it were two lancet-shaped windows, both of which depicted religious scenes – one of which appeared to show a saint ascending to heaven. Above them had been placed a circular window of sorts, which was made up of nine sections, which were separated by some rather tasteful stonework. Of the nine, the four corners – if you can have such a thing in a round window – appeared merely decorative, containing triangles of blue which were bordered on each side by strips of white glass. The other five panels were filled with symbols. The top center one contained a dove, which I knew had a raft of biblical associations, while the left and right featured the Greek letters Alpha and Omega. The bottom center contained the letters I H C and the middle section, by far the largest of the nine, featured a Templar cross on a white shield.

I asked Holmes about the meaning of the bottom panel and he explained that the letters IHC were often used as a pictograph to represent the name Jesus.

He continued staring up at the window and finally said, "I'm going to need a ladder. Perhaps there is one in the outbuilding; if not, we must hope that someone in the village can provide one."

A trip to the outbuilding proved fruitless, so we ventured into the village – if such it can be called. There were perhaps four or five houses, and they were all a good distance from one another. We stopped at the first house we came to but our knocks went unanswered. At the second house, a man answered. He was tall and thin with a shock of dark hair and he seemed wary of strangers.

Holmes introduced us and then explained that we were antiquarians looking into the history of the Temple Church.

After introducing himself as Joseph Wojno, the man said, "Do you mean the Church of St. Catherine?"

"Indeed," Holmes replied, "but as I said we are historians looking into the origins of the church which was founded by the Knights Templar."

"You know it was rebuilt just over a decade ago? Never could understand it myself, pouring all that money into a church that gets used only a few times a year." Gesturing around, he said, "As you can see there's no congregation here to support a pastor – let alone a church."

"Well, I wanted to examine the workmanship in the stained glass windows, and I was wondering if you might have a ladder we could borrow."

"You'll not damage it nor the church?" he inquired.

"You have my word," replied Holmes, and I'll even leave you a deposit of £5 if you'd like."

"That should do," said the man. Then he stopped, paused for a few seconds and asked, "How did you get into the church? I thought it was all locked up."

"We obtained the key from the dean at St. Petroc's Church in Bodmin," Holmes lied smoothly.

The answer seemed to satisfy Wojno, who led us to a small barn, from which he retrieved a 12-foot ladder. "'Tis the only one I have, so I hope it's high enough," he said.

"This will do splendidly," replied Holmes. Then he, Green and I carried the heavy wooden ladder back to the church. We brought it to the rear wall and leaned it over the altar, which was bare of all cloths and holy implements at the time. Holmes ascended the ladder while Green and I steadied it. Holmes then took out his lens and proceeded to examine every aspect of the window quite closely.

At one point, he called down, "Correct me if I'm wrong but I believe the Latin word for hours is *horae* – h-o-r-a-e," he said spelling out each letter, "is it not?"

"Indeed it is," replied Green. "The singular would be *hora*, without the e."

"Well, then this will either be quite simple or quite difficult, it all depends," he said. He then returned the lens to his pocket and withdrew a pencil and paper. I watched as he scanned the window and made a note. After repeating this process, several times, he said, "I think I have it, but I'm not quite certain what it is I have."

"May I examine the window, Mr. Holmes?" asked Green.

"No need, Captain. Trust me when I tell you I've seen everything there is to see. Besides, it is getting rather late, and I don't want to be driving across the moor in darkness."

However, Green was not to be dissuaded and no sooner had Holmes stepped off the ladder then he began his ascent.

Holmes had a look of exasperation on his face, and when he glanced at me, I could do nothing but shrug my shoulders. After Green had concluded his own examination he descended, and Holmes then handed him a sheet of paper he had been holding.

"I trust you saw the carvings, and arrived at the same conclusion as I."

"I did, Mr. Holmes."

Speaking more to me now, Holmes continued, "Like those in the outbuildings, the stones that make up the frame surrounding the window appear to be much older than those around them. In fact, I wouldn't be surprised if that section of this wall is the original workmanship. At any rate, in one of the pieces near the base of the window, I found the word *horae* inscribed. It was quite faint and difficult to discern, so to satisfy myself I made a tracing." With that he held up the paper and we could just see ever so faintly the Latin word for hours.

"With *horae* as a clue, I began to search the other stones for marks. Again, they were faint and almost indecipherable, but they survived. See if you can make anything out of it." On the page were seven symbols:

▽ ∨ ▷ ◊ ◁ ◊ ∧

"I noticed those but as they were separated I thought nothing of them," said Green. Then glancing at the paper, he continued, "As they are written here, they spell out nothing."

"Nothing?" replied Holmes.

"Tell me, what letters do you see."

"The letters are L, I, A, C, M, H, E," said Green.

"If it's straightforward, you should be able to crack it in an hour or two," I said.

Suddenly, Green spoke up, "There are seven symbols; the Benedictines observed seven holy hours or times of prayer each day."

"Were any of those holy hours considered more important than the others?" asked Holmes.

"Yes, three in the afternoon, was called *None*; it is generally believed that is the time that Christ died."

"What were the others?" I asked.

"A Templar's day started quite early, usually around 4 a.m. when he would pray at what we call *Lauds*. At 5 a.m. or daybreak, the knights would observe *Prime* and they would pray and attend mass. Then came *Tierce* at 6 a.m., *Sext* at noon, *None* at 3 p.m., *Vespers* at 6 p.m. and *Compline* at bedtime."

"Yes, well done." said Holmes. "Now, let us begin at *None*, so then the first letter would be M, and after that the letters may appear mixed, but if you then place the various hours in alphabetical order, following the M and continue along, they spell out Michael."

"My word, Holmes, that's wonderful!" I exclaimed.

"Child's play," he remarked.

"Having made that discovery, do you think they split up the treasure or was it all transported to Mount St. Michael?" asked Green.

"I have no way of knowing, but I have not seen any indications that anything has been concealed here, so I'd suggest that we spend the night at the inn, and then make arrangements to try to head south tomorrow morning."

"What about the people who are following us? Is there any way we can throw them off the track?"

"An excellent point, Watson. Why don't you and Captain Green return the ladder to Mr. Wojno? I want to sit here and mull things over. I am very concerned with the actions of our adversaries, and perhaps I can devise a way to elude them."

Green took the front of the ladder and I lifted the rear. As we left the church, I was surprised to see the sun was sitting low in the sky. I looked at my watch and was stunned to see it was almost half five.

We returned the ladder to Wojno, who in turn returned the £5. I pushed a sovereign into his hand for his trouble, thanking him as I did so.

During our return to the church, Green and I wracked our brains but neither of us could devise any scheme that would throw our adversaries off the scent. As we neared the church, I called out for Holmes, but there was no answer. "He must be wrapped up in a world of his own," I said to Green. "When he is deep in thought, he sometimes loses track of everything – including the outside world."

We then entered the church, but there was no one inside. We made a quick circuit of the outbuildings and then reentered the church. With a sense of dread, I began to look everywhere. I knew if it were possible Holmes would have left me a sign of some sort.

Suddenly I saw it. One of the last rays of the setting sun had caught it and caused it to sparkle.

My heart was in my throat, for there it sat propped against the back wall of the church on the altar. The last time I had seen that silver cigarette case without its owner had been on a ledge high atop the Reichenbach Falls. It had been used to weigh down three pages from Holmes's notebook in which he described how Moriarty had let him compose the letter before they entered that final fatal "discussion of those questions which lie between" them.

My heart had been broken that day when I believed the "best and wisest man whom I had ever known" had perished at the foot of the falls along with his arch enemy.

I approached the altar with the same trepidation that had gripped me that fateful day in Switzerland. As I lifted the case, I saw there were no papers beneath it on the altar. My heart was torn between relief and confusion.

Had Holmes seen his abductors coming and left this here before they arrived? Had he gone out to meet them, hoping they wouldn't search the church and discover the cigarette case?

I was a walking maelstrom of emotions. I didn't know how, where, why or what had happened to my friend; all I knew was Sherlock Holmes was gone.

Part II – The Knights' Tale

December 1312-January 1313

Chapter 15

Sir Geoffrey stood silently on the tower in what seemed an endless vigil to his men. For two days, with only a few hours of sleep when exhaustion had finally overtaken him, he had remained there gazing northward. Through pouring rain and biting wind, he had kept a lonely watch, remaining motionless, gazing north for hours on end. His men had brought him food and drink though most of it remained untouched.

They had been at the Temple Church on Bodmin Moor for nearly a week, and in the days before they had departed from Hertfordshire, rumours had run rampant. Every peddler and itinerant knight who had entered the town brought news: The Pope had excommunicated all Templars; King Edward had ordered the Templars arrested and executed; King Edward had seized all the Templar lands and possessions, including the London Temple; King Edward was in league with King Philip of France. Truth was an elusive commodity.

In recent months, many of their brothers had fled England and sought refuge in Scotland and Ireland where, it is said, they were welcomed. Others had escaped to Portugal where it was well-known that King Denis had received them and promised them sanctuary.

Geoffrey wasn't certain what to believe, but he had received a secret communiqué from his master, Sir William de la More, the grand commander of the Templars in England, to gather whatever treasure he might lay his hands on and seek refuge at the Temple Church in Cornwall. He had followed his orders and gathered up two chests of precious stones, three more of gold coins and all the letters of credit his church had been holding for merchants and monarchs alike.

That had been nearly four weeks ago on the 3rd of December, 1312. Despite the cold weather, they had been able to secure enough provisions and what they lacked they had purchased on the way – sometimes at exorbitant prices. They had arrived, secured the church and tower as best they might and then begun waiting.

The birth of Our Lord had been celebrated in an understated manner and life went on much as before with prayer, fasting and self-mortification. He wondered about the men and how much longer their resolve would last in the face of an uncertain future – and an apparently vengeful monarch.

Geoffrey heard the rider long before he saw him. In the still of the evening, most of his men were all abed while he maintained his lonely watch. From the sound of it, the horse was moving at a full gallop. Finally, off in the distance, he spied a single rider making for the church. He was wearing a dark cloak which concealed his tunic, so Geoffrey couldn't tell if he were a knight or simply a messenger.

When the rider was perhaps two hundred yards from the church, he began to yell: "We are betrayed! Brothers, we are betrayed!"

Geoffrey recognized the voice as that of Peter of Chiselworth, a trusted lieutenant of William de la More. Geoffrey went down to meet the rider, and as he descended, he was aware that Peter's cries had awakened several members of the brotherhood.

In front of the church, Peter pulled up. Jumping from his steed, he said to Geoffrey. "All is lost, old friend."

"Slowly," said Geoffrey, "begin at the beginning and tell me all you know."

"I am pursued," said Peter, "so speed is essential."

"By whom?" asked Geoffrey.

"The King's army under the command of Sir Douglas of Deering."

"But Sir Douglas is one of us," said a voice in the darkness.

"Was! Was one of us," replied Peter bitterly. "For a pardon and the restoration of his title of Duke of Cornwall and all that comes with it, he has betrayed us all."

"At least he wasn't cheaply bought, but more of that later," said Geoffrey. "What says Sir William?"

"He says nothing," replied Peter. "My master is dead." At that he crossed himself and then continued, "He

167

died on the 20th of December in the Tower. Whether he was executed, succumbed to torture or simply died of a broken heart after the King showed his true colours, no one can say for certain. I must say Edward II was loath to take any action against the Order and he initially resisted following in the footsteps of King Philip. Eventually, however, he accepted the inquisitors and allowed them to sit in judgment of the order at the church of All Hallows by the Tower."

"Let us not forget that King Edward is engaged to the French monarch's daughter, and I'm certain he would sacrifice a great deal, including all of us, to maintain that alliance," said another of the men.

That brought murmurs from the rest of the company, both knights and sergeants. In order to ward off any more unpleasantness, Geoffrey seized control of the conversation, steering it back to the more pressing matters at hand. "Did Sir William send a message?" he asked.

"Aye, right up until the end he was able to see visitors who carried his commands to the other leaders."

"And what did Sir William wish me to do?"

"As his last request, he instructed me to tell you to take whatever steps you deemed necessary, but the treasure was not to fall into the hands of Edward or any of his men. As William put it, 'Tis a petty thing, but it is the least I can do.'"

"Did he give any specific orders besides those?" asked Geoffrey.

"He asked that you pray for his soul and remain true to your vows."

"And Sir Douglas? He knows we are here?"

"Aye, unfortunately he is not the only traitor. William learned the King has ordered the arrest of all the Templars in Britain and Ireland. He has secretly dispatched troops to all our churches, and our men are to be taken into custody starting on the 9th of January. He was hoping that by doing nothing for a month he might lull everyone into a false sense of security and then spring the trap starting next month. It also allows him time to move his men into position to make the arrests."

"Have we any loyal men left, or are we the last of the faithful?"

"I'm sure there are loyal men, but who they are, I cannot say. No one is standing up and proclaiming, 'I am a Templar.' And who can blame them?"

"You are right, but we must leave a message in the event that any who may come seeking allies and wish to join us know where to find us."

"What will you do, Sir Geoffrey?" asked one of his other lieutenants, Sir Lionel.

"I will leave a message – vague so that it will not be readily apparent but discernible for those willing to think and sacrifice a bit of time attempting to decipher it." Calling to one of his men, Geoffrey ordered, "Bring me a ladder. I will be in the church." To the rest of his men, Geoffrey ordered, "Prepare to ride. We leave within the hour."

After he was alone in the church, Geoffrey climbed the ladder and inscribed his message, using a chisel to engrave the letters of the secret alphabet of the Templars. He looked at the window and envisioned a clock. In order to confuse anyone who might just stumble upon it, he placed the first letter of the second word of the message at *None* or three in the afternoon and worked from there. The chisel flew as he chipped at the stone and he was done in about twenty minutes.

Looking at his work, he thought, "It's not much, but it is the best I can do." Then he said a final prayer and left the church.

As he was opening the door it struck him that he needed a way – a very subtle method – to draw attention to his message. And then inspiration hit him. With the hilt of his dagger he broke a small stained glass window in the sacristy and then he placed small pieces on the altar in the shape of the Greek letter Alpha. "Hopefully, they will see the symbol here and raise their eyes to God for guidance to decipher its meaning."

When he had finished, he placed the ladder in the courtyard and met his men who were now gathered in front of the church.

One of the men said, "I don't understand why we don't stay and fight them here. Food is plentiful, and there is little cover for them."

"What you say is certainly true," replied Geoffrey, "but I am certain they will come in great numbers, and we are but twenty. They can surround us and wait us out, and should their patience wear thin, those doors wouldn't stand up to a battering ram for very long – if at all. No, we will go south to Mount St. Michael. I admit we run the risk of being cut off there as well, but I think the sea may prove more our friend than theirs. Let us pray that I am right."

The men departed in the dead of night, but before he left, Geoffrey quickly drew a map that led to St. Winnow and thence to Fowey. He left it in his room on the floor under his bed next to his prie-dieu. "Perhaps, God willing, they will stumble across this as well. It may buy us some extra time." He then said a brief prayer and headed out to lead his men.

The journey south took them through Bodmin where Geoffrey told the innkeeper they were heading for the coast. They then followed a road that curved east in the general direction of the River Fowey. After about ten miles, they changed direction and started heading southwest again.

They rode for four more hours, stopping occasionally to rest the horses, eat and pray. After they had finished the prayer for *Prime*, one of the men pointed out, "We missed the prayer for *Lauds*."

Geoffrey smiled at the young man and said gently, "I believe God will understand if we are forced to miss a few prayers under the circumstances. We can always make them up when we reach Mount St. Michael."

As they rested in the field, Geoffrey recalled his own youth. His Uncle George had been a Templar and fought in the last crusade, under the leadership of Prince Edward of England and Charles of Anjou, the brother of Louis IX of France.

He had thrilled to the story of how they had killed the assassins, who posing as Christians seeking to convert and receive the sacrament of baptism, had attempted to murder Prince Edward. As he sat rapt listening to his uncle's many tales of battling the Mamluks and Saracens and hearing of the heroism demonstrated by the Templars, Geoffrey, though a mere lad of ten, had decided then and there that his future was to join the order. For as long as he could remember that had been his chosen fate.

Fortunately, as the third son, his father had no objections when he informed him of his choice. His mother, however, was not at all pleased. Truth be told, he had always been her favourite. Although she had her misgivings, she was slowly being won over until she found out that the Templar code forbade him from kissing all women – even her. She had pleaded her case with him on one occasion and when he remained resolute, she had resigned herself to a life of suffering in silence.

Between his reverie and his exhaustion, Geoffrey must have dozed off while riding. Suddenly he was awakened as one of his men exclaimed, "There she is – Mount St. Michael."

"Protect us, St. Michael, for we do the Lord's work. Guide my steps and aid my decisions," he prayed.

The weary knights arrived in the village of Marazion, and Geoffrey dispatched another of his lieutenants, Frederick, to find the mayor.

A few minutes later, Frederick returned leading a small, thin man whom he introduced as Simon Carlyon. The mayor bowed and then asked, "How may I be of service, Your Lordship?"

"My men and I must make our way to the monastery of Mount St. Michael," said Geoffrey.

"The monastery has long been deserted," replied the mayor. "No one has been there for as long as I've been alive."

"We need a quiet place to pray, reflect, and do penance," said Geoffrey.

"Then the island will do you fine."

"Do you have boats that can carry us there?"

"Aye, with all the fishermen in this town, boats are the last thing you need concern yourselves with."

"We'll also need to stock up on provisions and water," replied Geoffrey. "We may be there for some time."

"Take what you need," the mayor said. "The village is always happy to help the Order."

"We will pay a fair price for whatever we take," replied Geoffrey. "While we do appreciate your offer, your people work hard and they should not toil in vain."

Within a few hours, they had purchased enough provisions to last at least a month, including barrels of fresh water and a hogshead of wine. They made arrangements to have their horses looked after, and by late afternoon, they had all been transported to the island.

They climbed the hill to the fortress at the top, and Geoffrey thought with a little luck, they could hold out here indefinitely. He then turned his mind to Sir Douglas. "I have no idea how many men he is bringing, but I have nineteen brave lads who have followed me without questions, all of whom believe our cause is just."

After *Vespers*, they gathered for dinner. When they had eaten their simple meal of bread, beef and water, Geoffrey said, "Men, we must make plans. As you know we are being pursued. If my attempts at misdirection worked, we have at most a week before they arrive. If they didn't, Sir Douglas and his men could be here on the morrow." Turning to Sir Lionel, he said, "We have an unencumbered view of the shore, I want you to arrange a schedule so that we have lookouts posted at all times who will let us know the moment they see anything suspicious.

"We also need to set up buckets to catch any rainwater that we can, and those of you who have the knack may want to try your hand at fishing during your spare time. Obviously, we will soon be cut off, so our provisions must last as long as possible.

"Finally, we must guard the treasure so that it does not fall into their hands."

"They can just wait us out, sir," said William, a sergeant.

"True, that is why I have developed a plan which we will employ if all else fails." He then set about telling them what he would do with the treasure, and when he had finished, they could hardly contain themselves.

"Brilliant, sir! Blo- Absolutely brilliant!" exclaimed Peter, another of the sergeants, cutting himself off before the mild oath slipped out. "The old habits are the hardest to break," he said sheepishly. "I will pray to Our Lord for forgiveness."

"And while you are seeking absolution, please say a prayer or two for the rest of us. I have the feeling we are going to need it."

Chapter 16

For the next three days, life on the island was almost idyllic. The men went about their duties just as if they had been home in Hertfordshire. Each morning, two men rowed to the village in order to add to their stockpile of supplies. Each afternoon they returned in two different boats, having purchased an additional boat to add to their small fleet. On the second day they even returned with a rooster and three hens as one of the men planned to gather the eggs and hopefully raise the fowl on the island.

Early in the afternoon of the fifth day, there was a loud "Halloa" from one of the watchers. The other sentry quickly hastened to Geoffrey yelling as he ran, "There are men gathering on the beach, sir."

Geoffrey sprinted to the top of the battlements. The day, thankfully, was clear and in the distance he could just make out men as big as ants setting up camp along the shoreline. "How many archers do we have?" he asked, knowing the answer would be disappointing.

"Just the one," replied the sentry. "Dylan from Cardiff in Wales. However, he is quite an excellent archer and seldom misses what he aims at," added the sentry.

"Find him and send him to me. I will take your watch until you return."

A few minutes later, a tall, lanky Welshman stood in front of Geoffrey, who said, "I am told you are proficient with your bow."

"Whatever small degree of skill I may possess is a gift from God. What is it you need, my lord?"

Geoffrey then told him what he would like done and when he had finished, he looked at the archer and said, "Can you do that?"

"If I can find the materials here, and I believe I can, it should be relatively easy. If I cannot locate exactly what I need, I shall do my best to improvise."

"Do your best, that is all I ask," Geoffrey said.

"I will, my lord."

Geoffrey thanked the man, and then he rounded up Sir Lionel and Peter and began the steep descent to the shoreline. "Why are they here?" asked Peter.

"To arrest us and to find the treasure and return it to King Edward," answered Sir Lionel.

As they reached the short cliff right above the beach, they saw a boat push off from the shore and begin rowing towards them. Peter looked at Geoffrey and said, "You expected this?"

"Of course, it's exactly what I'd do."

About ten minutes later, the boat was thirty feet from shore. Geoffrey shouted out, "That's close enough. There's no need for you to come ashore."

In the boat, a tall elegant-looking man stood up, pushed back his hood and doffed his cloak. He then turned around to reveal the white tunic with the red cross signifying him as a member of the Knights Templar. Now facing Geoffrey, he said, "Is that any way to greet an old friend, Sir Geoffrey?"

"Good afternoon, Sir Douglas, how may I help you?" said Geoffrey.

"May we sit at a table like civilized men and discuss things? I come in peace with an offer of amnesty from the King."

"Do you have that in writing?" replied Geoffrey.

"I don't have the documents with me, but that is easily rectified once things have been settled."

"And what exactly is there to settle?"

Sir Douglas continued, "As you well know Pope Clement V dissolved the Order several months ago. All of the property and monetary assets have been seized by the monarchs of the various countries who plan on turning them over to the Knights Hospitallers."

"And what is it that you want from us?"

"You are to surrender this island immediately. We have already seized Hertfordshire, the church on Bodmin Moor and all the other holdings throughout England. You are the last recalcitrants."

"And what happens to us if we do as you wish?"

"You will confess your sins, receive absolution and resume your lives – perhaps as peasant farmers or perhaps as a member of some other order."

"Anything else?"

"You must turn over whatever property you have that belongs to the King."

"And what property might that be?"

"The safe-room was empty at Hertfordshire, and we found no treasure at Bodmin. King Edward wants what is rightfully his."

"And there's the rub," said Geoffrey. "The treasure you speak of does not belong to King Edward; it belongs to the Order."

"But the Order is no more!" exclaimed Douglas.

"Can a mere paper by a corrupt pontiff and a dithering monarch dissolve a way of life? I think not," said Geoffrey.

"I'll overlook the heresy – and the treason – this time," said Douglas. "Just give me what I want and we can go our separate ways. King Edward need not know we ever met."

"Nor ever see his treasure," thought Geoffrey.

"Give me twenty-four hours to discuss it with my men. Then let us meet here at this time tomorrow, and I will give you my decision."

Geoffrey watched as Douglas and his men rowed back to the beach. Leaving one man to sound the alarm in case they should decide to return, Geoffrey strode back up the steep path and then called all his men together in the small courtyard. After they had gathered, he relayed the demands Sir Douglas had delivered. When he had finished, he heard mumbling and grumbling among his men. He looked at them and said, "I will leave you to discuss it. Let us meet back here in half an hour and see what course of action we may follow."

He then left his men and strolled about the island taking in its natural beauty and wondering how his world had changed so drastically in such a short time. When he returned to the courtyard some forty minutes later, he asked quietly, "Have you been able to arrive at any sort of decision?"

Sir Lionel stood up and said, "We all took vows, and those vows mean something to us. We have dedicated our lives to God – not King Edward and certainly not Sir

Douglas. We will follow you, sir, and be guided by your counsel."

"You understand once we do this, we are outlaws."

"Better an outlaw than a sinner," one of the men exclaimed. At that they all laughed.

"Do you have a plan, sir?" asked Peter.

"I do, but I'm afraid it is not much of one. Obviously, we cannot remain here. Our supplies will run out eventually – something Sir Douglas need not concern himself with. We have enough boats hidden on the far side of the island. Hopefully, Sir Douglas is unaware of their presence. While we could stay and see how things develop, I propose we set sail tonight for St. Govan's Chapel in Wales. If we need to, we can put in at various villages along the shore and replenish our supplies. Once we have arrived in Wales, we can rest and then set sail for Ireland. I understand that many of our brethren have already found refuge there, and perhaps we may as well, God willing."

"That's a perilous journey, sir," said one of the men, "especially at this time of year."

"God's truth," said another, "and a long one too – especially in those boats."

Geoffrey paused, "I didn't say it was a good plan, but I think it better than the alternative. As most of you know, our master, William de la More, is dead. He was taken to the Tower where after some time he gave up the ghost. I cannot say for certain if he was tortured, but I believe he was. At any rate, I imagine his stay there was not a pleasant one."

"And what of the treasure?" asked a voice from the rear. "What shall we do with that?"

"It is not ours to keep," said Geoffrey. "We shall take enough to cover our expenses."

"And what of the rest?" asked Peter.

"I have a plan for that," replied Geoffrey. "Again, I do not know if you will approve of it, but it is the best my poor brain can come up with on such short notice."

"Would you care to share it with us?" asked Lionel.

When he had told them what he planned to do, they laughed and all agreed it was a brilliant idea.

"Now, I need three volunteers to help with the construction." Although every man offered his services, he selected his lieutenant, Peter; Dylan, the archer from Wales; and John, one of the younger members. He then told everyone else, "Go, gather your belongings and prepare to leave. We will set sail under cover of darkness tonight."

Geoffrey and John then began to scour one half of the island while Peter and Dylan covered the other. After two hours they met on the far side of the island, on a ledge above the beach overlooking the open sea rather than the village of Marazion. Below them on the shore sat the five small boats they would use to effect their escape.

As they worked, the fruits of their labor slowly began to take shape. "You know there are other things we could do with the treasure," said John.

"Agreed," replied Geoffrey, "but I think this is the most certain and certainly the most deceptive." He then explained the finishing touch, and the three of them laughed once again, marveling at Geoffrey's ingenuity.

After they had prayed, they returned to their toil with a new sense of purpose. As one might expect, they encountered a few setbacks along the way, but eventually their task was completed.

As they stepped back, Dylan said, "It's not much to look at, but I think it will do the job."

Having given the completed project one more close examination, Peter suggested they test it. "Better to know our shortcomings now, then when it matters."

They all agreed and sent John back to their camp. Perhaps ten minutes later he returned with the item requested. When it had been secured, they gave it a trial run, and to no one's surprise, it performed perfectly.

"Now, with a little good fortune, we just might be able to pull this off," thought Geoffrey.

Geoffrey then dismissed the men, ordering them to get some rest. Once alone, he set about putting the trickiest part of his plan into action. It was hard work since he lacked the proper tools but eventually he finished and thought, "With a bit of luck, this just might work."

As he returned to camp, he felt a stiff breeze on his back. Looking to heaven he said, "I can but hope that my will is Thy will."

At the campsite, he enjoyed a quiet dinner with his men immediately after *Vespers*.

Things had been going along quite smoothly and everything had been falling into place when suddenly Geoffrey saw the one thing which could upset all of his careful planning. Off in the distance, a bolt of lightning lit up the sky. Shortly afterwards, there was a loud clap of thunder. He knew the storm would be upon them soon enough.

Hoping against hope and knowing it was a selfish plea, he lifted his eyes towards heaven and said fervently, "Not tonight, Lord, please not tonight." Then remembering the words of Jesus in the Garden of Gethsemane, he added, "Not my will but yours be done."

Moments later Geoffrey knew that his prayers, much like those of his Lord and Saviour's, were going to go unanswered as the rain started to fall and the wind began to pick up.

He watched as lightning rent the darkened sky and thunder boomed almost immediately after. "Perhaps it will pass quickly," he thought. But three hours later, the rain was still coming down in torrents and the wind had increased to a screeching howl.

"If this is an omen, I don't like it," said Peter.

"Nor I," replied Geoffrey, "but I fear our course is set and there's no turning back at this late juncture."

Offering another prayer, he took one more look at the roiling sea and then turned to where the tree branches were bending under the gusts of wind. "Perhaps this is God helping us," he thought.

Chapter 17

"Perchance, we'll be able to remain here tonight and then set sail tomorrow night," suggested Peter.

"Perhaps," replied Geoffrey, "but double the watch just in case Sir Douglas hopes to catch us napping and decides to pay us a visit tonight."

"Do you really think he would do that?"

"It's exactly what I'd do if the circumstances were reversed."

Geoffrey called the men into the refectory of the monastery. He then explained to them that the plans were far from set in stone. "I should have liked to have set sail tonight – and we still may if it becomes necessary – but I'd prefer to depart in calmer weather. If Sir Douglas attacks, we will sound the alarm, and you must be prepared to go at a moment's notice. If he holds off, and God willing he will, then we will set sail tomorrow night.

"So now, let us pray and then each of you should try to get some rest. Whether we leave tonight or tomorrow, it's going to be a long, rough voyage and I will need all of you ready and sharp."

Geoffrey knew he wouldn't sleep, for he was too tense with apprehension to allow rest to overtake him. Finally, after two hours he dozed off but his respite was short-lived. He heard men yelling and then he was being shaken. "They are coming, Sir Geoffrey," John said. "The watch just caught a glimpse of sails in the distance."

"Are they certain?"

"As sure as anyone can be in this weather," replied John.

"Go find Dylan and tell him to meet me at the shoreline where they arrived earlier. Send Peter and Lionel to me and then gather the rest of the men and have them wait on the cliff above the boats."

Two minutes later, Peter and Lionel entered Geoffrey's room.

"Have you the chests?" asked Geoffrey, and when they replied in the affirmative, he said, "Here is the key, I think you know what to do."

After picking up a sword and a small metal container with the embers of the fire, Geoffrey left and started running hard toward the shoreline. Perhaps five minutes later he arrived. He saw Dylan standing there waiting for him and in a flash of lightning, he saw two white sails in the distance. "I've brought the embers," Geoffrey explained.

"Good! I've prepared several of my arrows, and I have a small jar of oil. As to the rest, I've already made all my preparations. When they get in range – perhaps another three minutes, I'll take the shots. Hope for more lightning as it will make my task all the easier."

"Can you do this without killing any of them? After all, his men are Christians, not Saracens, and they are merely following orders," said Geoffrey.

"I will aim for the sails, my lord, as we discussed, but with the rain and the wind, I can make no promises."

"Just do your best, Dylan."

By now they could see the sails of two different boats with what looked like another two or three a short distance behind them. Each boat looked as though it carried between ten and twenty men. The closest ones, which were the two largest, were about 100 yards from shore. Dylan pulled an arrow from his quiver, doused the tip which he had swathed with a cloth in oil and lit it from the fire Geoffrey had brought. It burst into flame and he quickly nocked it, drew back the bow, aimed and released it. They watched as the arrow lit up the sky for a few brief seconds before flying over the mast of the first boat and falling harmlessly into the bay.

Even before the first arrow had finished its flight, Dylan had loosed a second and this time his aim was true. It struck near the top of the mast of the lead boat and despite the rain, the sail began to burn. He quickly fired four more arrows, three hit their marks, striking the first two boats, and the fourth fell harmlessly into the bay.

"Those were all the flaming arrows, I had prepared," he said ruefully, but the boats were already heading back towards the town. "You have done well," said Geoffrey. "Now it's almost time for us to set sail, but first a little fun – at King Edward's expense."

They quickly made their way across the island to the side away from the town where they found the men admiring the fruits of their labour from the afternoon.

"Does it work?" one of the men asked.

"We tested it this afternoon," replied Sir Geoffrey, "but now comes the real test. Bring me the first chest." When he opened it, the men were surprised to see that it had been filled with small rocks and pebbles. Two men carried it to Geoffrey and he told them, "Take half the stones and put them in the basket." They did as they were ordered, and then Geoffrey said, "Much of the credit for this belongs to Dylan, so I think he should have the honor of the first real test."

Dylan stepped to the machine, pulled out his dirk and cut the rope. With an audible whoosh, the basket flew straight up to a 90-degree angle while the stones went flying far out into the sea. "I think it works," said Dylan with a smirk.

"I wish King Edward and Sir Douglas good fortune in trying to recover those," said Sir Lionel.

The catapult had been pulled back into position and the remainder of the stones were emptied into the basket.

Geoffrey instructed the men to switch the angle and then Sir Lionel cut the rope and a second batch of rocks flew through the air landing somewhere out at sea.

They followed suit three more times with baskets of rocks, each time moving the catapult and aiming at a different section of the darkened sea. Within fifteen minutes, they had completed their task and proceeded to chop apart the catapult.

"Hopefully, they will see the remains of the catapult and figure out what we have done," said Lionel.

"I'm going to give them some help," replied Geoffrey. So saying, he opened his purse and pulled out a handful of gold coins which he scattered along the ledge. Then by the ruined catapult, he dropped a few more coins among the debris as well as two diamonds and a ruby.

They then descended to the beach, climbed into their boats and prepared to set out on the heaving obsidian sea for St. Govan's Chapel, a distance of more than one hundred miles. Though the cautious might have waited another day in hopes of better weather, Sir Geoffrey – badly outnumbered as he was – did not want to risk a confrontation with Sir Douglas under any circumstances. "Better to run away and live to fight another day," he thought. Another factor in his decision was he loathed the idea of taking up arms against his fellow Christians.

With a heavy heart, Geoffrey ordered his men to push off from shore and set sail for Wales.

For all intents and purposes, that small group of Knights Templar might as well have dropped off the face of the Earth that night. What became of them? Who can say? All that is known for certain is they were never heard from again.

Part III – A Return to Watson

Chapter 18

I fought to bring my emotions under control – no easy task. Then I turned to Green and said, "Perhaps Holmes decided to leave immediately for the Old Inn." Although I didn't believe a word I had just uttered, I was determined not to fall into a pit of despair.

After one more look around the grounds of the church, including the cemetery, we drove back to the inn in the gloaming. It was a long and bitter journey. I had already "lost" Holmes once; I wasn't certain if I could stand losing him twice.

When we finally arrived at our destination perhaps an hour and a half later – I must admit to pushing the horse rather hard – Broad came out into the courtyard to meet us and tend to the beast.

"I don't suppose you have seen Mr. Holmes?" I asked.

"Aye, he arrived about thirty minutes ago, rented my best stallion, and said I could get her back from O'Leary tomorrow when I drove you to Bodmin."

"He was here?" I asked, my heart in my throat. I cannot convey how relieved I was to hear this news.

"I just told ya he was; are ya deaf, man?"

"Did he leave a message of any kind?"

"Aye," he answered. Reaching into his pocket, he pulled out a sheet of paper which I saw Holmes had sealed with candle wax from the church, and handed it to me.

"He said I should tell you that you should read it over dinner, which Mrs. Broad has held for you."

Although I was desperate to open the missive, I decided to follow Holmes's instructions, so Green and I entered the dining room. Mrs. Broad had prepared a brace of game hens for us with potatoes and leeks. When she served them, she said, "My husband shot them only this morning."

The meal might have been the best I had ever eaten, but I don't think I tasted anything. As soon as Mrs. Broad had left the room, I pulled out the letter, broke the wax seal and began to read.

My Dear Watson,

I am sorry for any misgivings my sudden departure may have caused you. Please believe me when I say that causing you any distress was the last thing I wanted to do.

I made a second discovery in the church and felt that my presence in Mount St. Michael as soon as possible was of paramount importance. Tomorrow, I want you and Captain Green to make your way to the village of Marazion and book rooms in the nearby Godolphin Hotel. You may want to use aliases.

I shall be in touch as soon as I have something substantial to report. Keep your wits – and your Webley – about you.

    SH

The next morning, we awoke early and after a hearty breakfast, Broad drove Green and me to Bodmin. Perhaps three hours later, we arrived in that town and made our way to O'Leary's Stables. The owner greeted us and said, "I've been expecting you. Mr. Holmes said you'd be along presently."

"Is there a train from here to Marazion?" I asked.

"No, but there is a direct road."

"What's the distance?" I asked.

"About fifty miles," replied O'Leary.

As I was doing the math in my head trying to figure out how long it would take us when Green spoke up, "Is there a train from Bodmin to Penzance?"

"Of course," replied O'Leary.

"And how far from Penzance to Marazion?"

"Couldn't say exactly, but I'd guess it's only about five or six miles – certainly no more than ten."

We grabbed our bags, ran to the train station, and two hours later we were on our way to Penzance. My thoughts about Holmes's inexplicable behaviour were interrupted when Green asked me, "Have you any idea what might have occasioned Mr. Holmes's sudden departure?"

"Quite frankly, I am as in the dark as you, but I will tell you this: I know from experience Holmes frequently likes to act as a solo agent. As such, he is not hindered in any way. But at the same time, I genuinely think he values my occasional insights and he appreciates me as a sounding board. So while I am confused by his actions, I must admit I am not entirely surprised by them.

"He is a very private man with some singular gifts. Fortunately, he has chosen to fight on the side of the angels."

As we arrived in Penzance, I found myself humming the melody to Gilbert and Sullivan's "I Am the Very Model of a Modern Major-General." I had to smile in spite of myself as I recalled the enjoyable performance I had taken in at the Savoy some seven years earlier when the show had been revived.

We hired a cab and made our way to the Godolphin Hotel, which I learned was slightly more than five miles distant. It appeared the decision to take the train had been a good one.

When we arrived at the hotel, it was obvious the place had been remodeled in the not-too-distant past, and I learned that it had previously been called the Godolphin Arms. After we had secured rooms under the names Hudson and Wiggins, I decided to stroll about the town. Green offered to accompany me. I acquiesced since I had no reason for refusing, but secretly, I was hoping I might spot Holmes in one of his disguises.

Claiming to be the oldest town in Cornwall, Marazion, I soon discovered, was a place replete with legends and folktales. I have already mentioned the Jack and the Beanstalk tale, and I also learned of miracles that had allegedly been performed there in the late 13th century. It is also believed that in the late fifth century, a group of local fishermen saw St. Michael the Archangel standing on a ledge on the island – hence the name – in a place that became known as Michael's Chair. All told, it was as though I had stepped back in time.

Eventually, Green and I made our way down to the beach. As we looked out at the island of Mount St. Michael, I jokingly said, "I do hope the adventure ends there because we've run out of land if it hasn't."

I also saw that it really was possible to walk to the island across a causeway which had been first constructed in the early 15th century. However, if you wanted to use the causeway you had to coordinate your visit with the tides. I asked a local, "What happens if you walk out there and the tide comes in?"

He looked at me as if I were a bit simple, and then he said, "Ya might have to spend the night, unless you are fortunate enough to do it during the day in which case you can probably come back in a bit, but it'll cost ya."

I was considering a visit the next day – via boat – and Green said he'd be happy to accompany me. At dinner that night, I asked the waiter about going to the island, and he said, I could hire a boat for a few bob or try to walk it. He also said low tide, when the causeway would be exposed, was tomorrow afternoon. Wanting to get to the island as soon as possible, I decided to engage a boat and walk back if possible.

The next morning we made our way to the beach and for £2, the boatman agreed to ferry us over and for another £2, he would meet us and ferry us back at a time of our choosing. I suggested four o'clock and he agreed. "That should be more than enough time to take in the island and the castle," he offered.

He was an old codger with piercing blue eyes, a weathered face, and a head of iron-grey hair. During the short trip, he told us he had never set foot outside Cornwall and had never been more than ten miles from home. "The furthest I've ever been is Penzance," he informed us grandly.

As you might expect, he was a repository of local knowledge. While crossing to the island, which took only about ten minutes – as he preferred to row rather than use his sail – he told us about the St. Aubyn family who had owned the island for hundreds of years, and his chest puffed out with pride as he recalled the time Queen Victoria and her husband had visited the island "some fifty years ago now."

He dropped us off at a small pier, pointed to a path and said, "That'll take you to the top."

Looking up I saw an impressive building that might have served as the setting for *Ivanhoe*. I looked at Green and asked, "Is that the monastery?"

"He laughed and said, "No, the castle was built in the 15th century, no doubt using some of the stones from the original buildings. I believe the church and the monastery are still pretty much intact although I am certain both have been renovated over the years. So I don't know how much we can learn from them."

"Your point is well-taken," I said. "Still Holmes did manage to suss out the truth from the Temple Church on the moor."

I watched as Green took in his surroundings, and I realized the man was in his element. Suddenly he turned to me and asked, "Shall I tell you about the rich history and many myths associated with the tiny island of Mount St. Michael?"

"Perhaps tonight over dinner," I replied, "right now I want to scour the island to see if we can detect any sign of Holmes."

"Shall we do it together, or would you prefer to split up so that we can cover twice as much ground?"

"I think splitting up is an excellent idea." Pulling out my watch, I saw that it was half ten. "It's a small island, I think we should be able to traverse it both ways in about three hours. So if we meet back here at two o'clock we should have time to spare and then we can compare notes."

"Excellent," he replied, so when the path diverged about halfway up the hill, I went left while he continued on towards the castle. As I walked along, I was enjoying the fresh sea air and the warm sun on my face. I was looking for any sign of a campfire or indication that someone was sleeping rough, but after ninety minutes, I was back where I had started and had seen nothing. Undaunted, I continued up the path to the castle and the shops where I was able to refresh myself with tea and crumpets. Then it occurred to me that I might be able to have a view that encompassed the entire island if I could get to the battlements.

Thanks to our boatman, I knew the island and castle were owned by a family named St. Aubyn. I made my way to the main door of the castle, knocked and introduced myself. Fortunately, the young man who answered the door was a fan of my Holmes stories, and when I explained that I was working on a novel of historical fiction, he agreed to give me a quick tour. "Lucky for you the family is away right now," he said.

As we walked, he asked, "Will your book be anything like *Ivanhoe* or *The White Company* by that Doyle fellow?"

I explained that the book was still being researched, and I hadn't made any decisions about the plot or exact time period in which the action would occur.

He seemed satisfied, and when we reached the battlements, the view was stunning. However, a complete circuit revealed no signs of a campsite. The only things of note were the terraced gardens behind the castle and the presence of one or two stone crosses in rather remote areas. I wasn't completely surprised because I knew if Holmes didn't want to be discovered, he wouldn't be.

I met up with Captain Green where we had parted. He had little to add, so we made our way back to the jetty where our boatman was waiting for us. "I thought you might be early; three hours seemed overly generous," he said. "Once you've seen the castle and the gardens there's really naught else to keep you here."

We walked from the beach to the hotel – all the while I was looking for anyone who might have been Holmes in disguise. However, as might be expected, if he were operating incognito, his subterfuge was impeccable.

Back at the hotel, Green and I stopped in the dining room and enjoyed a pint. After a long, exhausting day, I decided a short nap before dinner was in order, so I arranged to meet Green in the dining room at half seven. I returned to my room after having instructed the front desk to rouse me at seven.

I had just fallen asleep – or so it seemed – when I heard a gentle rapping on the door, and a voice announced, "Dr. Watson, it's seven o'clock."

I roused myself, splashed some cold water on my face and dressed for dinner. The meal was a desultory affair. I will say that Green held up his end of the bargain admirably, and I am certain if I could have concentrated, I'd know a great deal more about the history and legends surrounding the isle of Mount St. Michael than I do.

The one thing I do remember is that in 1588 watchers on Mount St. Michael were supposedly the first ones to spot the approach of the Spanish Armada. They lit a torch which started a relay system. As a result, the English fleet in Plymouth had more than enough time to prepare for the engagement.

I returned to my room and after reading for a bit. I decided to turn in. As you can imagine, I was stunned to discover a small envelope had been concealed between the two pillows on my bed. I quickly tore it open and pulled out a sheet of paper.

On it were written six words and four symbols:

Remain silent and stay the course!

I recognized the spidery hand as Holmes's own and cursed him for always having to be so cryptic. The message was straightforward enough but what was he trying to convey with those crosses.

Then I wondered why he had neither addressed nor signed it, and then it hit me that he wanted no one – not even Green, obviously – to know that he was either in Marazion or close by.

I burned both the envelope and the note in the fireplace, stirring the ashes when I had finished.

I went to bed that night with my emotions once again in a state of turmoil. On the one hand, I was relieved to know that Holmes was well and nearby, but on the other I was annoyed that he seemed to feel he could not confide in me.

As you might expect, sleep was elusive. All I could think about were the crosses which Holmes had included on his letter. What was he trying to tell me? Was it yet another case of my seeing but not observing? I had passed one stone cross during my exploration of the island, and I was pretty certain that the one I had spied from the battlements was a different cross. I promised myself to look into it on the morrow.

I finally fell asleep what seemed like hours later, but my dreams were plagued by images of knights, crosses, Spanish galleons and an impending feeling of dread.

Chapter 19

I awoke the next morning with a clear idea of what I wanted to accomplish. I breakfasted with Green and announced my intention to return to the island.

"What do you hope to find there?" he asked.

"Truthfully, I am not certain, but I firmly believe the island in some way will figure prominently in this case. I'm not looking for anything in particular," I lied. "I'm just hoping to find something, some small indication that may prove helpful to Holmes when he rejoins us."

"Excellent," he replied. "Unless you believe I can be of help, I think I shall spend the day visiting Chysauster."

"What in heaven's name is that?" I asked.

"It's an ancient village, some six miles northwest of here which dates back to the later Iron Age. Apparently, it was still in use during the time of the Roman Empire. I've never seen it, but I'm told there are a number of round huts, the walls of which are mostly intact and apparently well-preserved. I should like to contrast it to the workmanship I saw in the Middle East – especially those early buildings that still survive in and around Jerusalem."

Once again, we agreed to meet for dinner at half seven and then went our separate ways. I made my way down to the small pier and found the same boatman, sitting there mending nets. "Going back again, are ya?"

"Yes, there are still a few things I'd like to explore further."

"Where's ya mate?"

"Oh, he had some business that required his attention, so I have a free day."

We set off and after a moment or two, he said, "If you like old things, you should visit St. Uny's Church in Lelant. Never seen it myself, but I'm told it's interesting. Still, I imagine it can't compare to our own Mount St. Michael."

After a few more suggestions of things I ought to see, we arrived at the jetty. "Same as yesterday?" he inquired.

"Yes, I'll meet you back here around four."

I began to explore the island looking for stone crosses. I wasn't exactly sure what I was looking for beyond that. I decided to see if anyone in the castle knew how many crosses there were and what might be their locations. Fortunately, I found the young man who had taken me to the battlements the previous day and asked him about any stone crosses on the island.

"There are four crosses I know of," he stated, "and they are all different." He then told me their names and where I might find them. He also drew me a rather crude map. I thanked him, handed him a few coins for his troubles, and set out on my way.

The first cross I came upon was called the Sinns Barton Cross. It was a lantern cross – so named because the top had been carved to resemble a lantern. On this one each face had been decorated with a different carving. It was standing on an outcrop of rock high on the northeast side of the island. I examined the carvings quite carefully and was wishing I had brought a lens. I then turned my attention to the ground all around it, but I could discern no signs of disturbance. I next proceeded to the Trevean Cross, a wheel-headed cross which I easily discovered in the midst of the gardens on the east side of the Mount. Again, a careful examination of the monument and the ground surrounding it revealed nothing.

Next I headed to the south side of the island, where I encountered the Mount St. Michael Cross, another wheel-headed marker. It stood on the edge of a high ledge below the castle. This one was slightly different from the other wheel-cross as it featured two crosses, one on the front and one on the rear. Below the cross on the front was carved a figure which I assumed was Jesus Christ and above the head in relief was a Maltese cross. I thought this one might be considerably older than the others I had seen, but I had no way of telling for certain.

My examination again proved fruitless, and I was glad to be heading for the fourth cross on the western side as the location of the Mount St. Michael Cross had given me some consternation. I am not at my best when dealing with heights.

Just as I made it safely to the next terrace, I heard a familiar voice ask, "Leaving so soon?"

I turned to discover Sherlock Holmes standing there, smoking a cigarette, as nonchalantly as can be. "I am glad you ascertained the meaning behind my message. You have done well, Watson. However, had you started with this cross, we might have had this conversation some forty minutes ago."

"Have you been following me?"

"All around this island," he laughed.

"But I never saw you."

"That may be because you weren't looking. You were too set upon your mission to examine the crosses and thus you ignored the people around you – never a good practice."

"But why meet me here and now?"

"Look around you. There is no one near us nor could anyone get within fifty yards of us without being seen. If ever a conversation had to be private, this is one."

"My word, Holmes. You are getting more secretive as you get older."

At that he chuckled and then asked, "By the by, where is Captain Green today?"

"He decided to visit the ancient village at Chysauster. He wanted to compare the ruins there to those he had explored on his travels through the Middle East."

"Does he know that you were coming here?"

"He does. We agreed to meet tonight for dinner at the hotel. Now, Holmes, it's my turn. What have you been up to since you disappeared at the Temple Church and what, if anything, have you learned?"

"I think I have nearly enough proof to bring this case to a close. It's just a question of how and when to ring down the curtain."

Holmes then proceeded to explain to me in great detail what he had been doing and what he had learned since we had parted ways on Bodmin Moor. When he had finished, I am certain my mouth was agape. Everything he said just seemed too incredible to be true. Still, I had one question that remained unanswered. "Have you located the treasure of the Templars?"

"I believe I can say with some degree of certainty that I have."

"And where is it?"

"We'll have time for that later. Right now, we have plans to make."

Holmes then outlined exactly what he wanted me to do. When he had finished, he said, "A great deal depends upon you, Watson. I must remain incommunicado for the next several days, during which time I am relying upon you to soldier on. You have never let me down before."

"And I shan't start now," I promised him.

"You still have you your pistol?"

I nodded, and then he added, "Don't go anywhere without it."

"What will you do right now?"

"I am returning to Penzance. I have a great deal more research to do and I'm hoping to find my answers in the Morrab Library there, but if my searches prove fruitless then I fear I must return to the British Library in London."

"Can no one here help you?"

"The historian with whom I would most like to speak is currently residing in the Bodmin Mental Asylum.

His name is John Thomas Blight. He is the author of *Ancient Crosses and Other Antiquities in the East of Cornwall*. Unfortunately, he suffered a complete mental breakdown some thirty years ago. I made an attempt to see him but was rebuffed by the family. They are very protective and understandably so."

"It seems as though everything conspires against us in this case," I remarked.

"That's certainly the truth," Holmes replied, "which will make our eventual triumph all the sweeter. Now I must go. I want to catch the low tide and return to Marazion via the causeway."

"Should I remain here?"

"You've agreed to meet your boatman at four, and I wouldn't want you to disappoint him. Take care, old friend."

"What am I to tell Green?"

"Oh, I am certain you will think of something."

With that he turned on his heel and headed towards the path that would bring him to the bay. It was only a few minutes later that it hit me: How did Holmes know when I was supposed to meet my boat?

I spent the rest of the day admiring the beauties of this gem of an island, and at four my boatman was waiting at the dock. As he rowed us back, he asked, "Did you have a productive day?"

I considered asking him about Holmes and then decided against it. If Holmes wanted to remain incommunicado, he was probably trying to maintain a low profile so the less attention I drew to him, the better.

"You could say that," I replied, and then we spent the next few minutes chatting about the fare at the Godolphin Hotel. He advised me in no uncertain terms to try the mussels for dinner. "They are all locally harvested, you know."

I walked back to the hotel where the clerk at the front desk called me over and said, "A man was inquiring after you earlier today, Mr. Hudson."

"Oh, did he say what his business was, or did he leave a note?"

"No note, but he did say to tell you he would be in touch."

"Do you recall what he looked like?"

"I'm sorry, sir, but I wasn't on duty when the inquiry was made. The message was passed to me and I was asked to relay it to you."

I took a quick look in the dining room, but as it was early, the room was empty.

I went up to my room wondering who it might have been. To the best of my knowledge, the only people who knew my whereabouts were Holmes and Green. Of course, there was still the mysterious man on the bridge in Hyde Park. He might have followed us here, and since he seemed to know quite a bit about Holmes, I thought it possible that he had divined my alias.

It was a conundrum but one that I am certain Holmes might have solved in mere minutes. Once I had settled myself in my room, I began composing my notes on this case. I've found that sometimes writing something out helps me to see it more clearly. After about two hours, I had made considerable progress with my notes but enlightenment continued to prove elusive.

When I finally ceased my labours, I looked at my watch and saw that it was almost time for supper. I went downstairs and found Green sitting at a table in the dining room. He looked eager to talk, and when I asked him how his day had been, he proceeded to tell me all about the huts that made up Chysauster.

"It is a most fascinating place," he enthused. He then began to recount his visit describing in some detail the stone-walled homesteads, which he said were also known as "courtyard houses." He added such structures could be found only on the Land's End peninsula and the nearby Isles of Scilly. He droned on about how the houses lined what might be described as a "street" and each had a central courtyard which in turn was surrounded by a number of thatched rooms.

I feigned interest as best I could, but my mind was definitely elsewhere. I looked around the room searching for strangers. Only two other tables were occupied. At one sat a young couple while the other had been taken by a solitary male patron who appeared to be at least seventy.

As I scanned the room, my thoughts kept returning to the crosses on the island. I suspected that once again Holmes had seen something which I had overlooked, or he had made one of those astounding leaps of logic that appeared beyond the ken of mere mortals such as myself.

All of a sudden I was roused back to consciousness when I heard Green say, "So, Doctor, what do you think?"

I stammered out an apology and confessed that my mind had been elsewhere as I was concerned about Holmes and preoccupied with the case.

"No need for apologies, Doctor, I know that I tend to prattle on incessantly once I have warmed to my subject. I was merely suggesting that if you have no plans for tomorrow, you might accompany me back to Chysauster. I figure as long as I'm here I might as well spend as much time there as I possibly can. I may not have another opportunity to conduct research of this nature for quite some time. So what do you say, would you care to step back in time with me tomorrow?"

I must admit that I was mildly intrigued, so I thanked him for his offer and agreed to accompany him to the ancient village for the day.

Chapter 20

Early the next morning, we rented a dog cart and set out for Chysauster. It was perhaps six miles from Marazion and the weather was cooperating. Slightly more than an hour later, we arrived at the village. There were the remnants of eight huts and as we walked among them, I kept thinking about the events of the past twenty-four hours.

Green, meanwhile, was busy examining the walls, the courtyards, and the construction of the various buildings. "These differ in many ways from the early structures I encountered in the Middle East," he informed me. I nodded and smiled but there was nothing about the ruins that I found engaging.

Finally, early in the afternoon, we decided to head back. We were about halfway home when we rounded a bend in the road and found two men on horseback blocking our way. They were masked and holding pistols aimed at us, and I thought we were about to be robbed.

However, one of the men pointed his gun at me and instead of demanding our valuables, asked, "Now then, Dr. Watson, or should I call you Mr. Hudson, where is Mr. Holmes?"

"I'm certain I do not know anyone named Holmes," I replied.

"Dr. Watson, you do yourself and me a disservice," he replied.

At that point I was pretty certain that I was listening to the man Holmes had encountered on the bridge in Hyde Park. "You!" I exclaimed.

"Ah, your memory has returned. The last time I saw you was when you were pretending to be a bum sleeping on a bench in Hyde Park."

"What is it that you want?"

"I don't think you were paying attention: I want to know where Holmes is."

"Obviously, you've been following me, so you should know he's not here."

At this point, out of the corner of my eye, I saw Green reaching for his pistol. Unfortunately so did the masked man. "Hold it right there, Captain Green, if you value your life."

Turning back to me, the man on horseback said, "Doctor, I saw you talking with Holmes on Mount St. Michael yesterday. So please do not try my patience: Where is Mr. Holmes today? Has he gone to seek out the treasure? Does he know where it is?"

"Holmes has returned to London," I lied smoothly. At which point it suddenly struck me that I was developing quite a gift for subterfuge. "He said there was something in the British Library he wanted to research. So no, he hasn't gone to seek the treasure, and if he knows where it is, he hasn't confided in me." I wondered if there were a real distinction between lying and equivocating. I finished with, "And before you ask, he didn't say when he would return."

"There now – that wasn't so difficult, was it?"

212

"Now, we are going ride away. I'd suggest you refrain from pulling your pistols or trying to stop us in any way. I brought my sniper with me for just such a situation."

With that they rode past us heading in the general direction of Penzance. As Green went to draw his pistol, I put my hand on his arm, "He may very well be telling the truth about the sniper. There was one in Hyde Park the night Holmes met with him on the bridge."

By this time they were around the bend and out of sight. "They can't be staying too far away, so I am pretty certain we will see them again – hopefully under more advantageous circumstances." I said.

"My word, that was nervy – and in broad daylight," spluttered a frustrated Green.

"Yes, but this is one of the most remote parts of the kingdom. These men have proved a fair match for Holmes so far, but I am certain their good fortune cannot continue."

"Should we inform the local constabulary?"

"To what end? We have no information to give them nor were there any witnesses."

We headed back to the hotel in silence, each of us lost in his own thoughts.

The next two days, Marazion was battered by rain and high winds. From my room at the front of the hotel I could see that on the first day no one was heading over to Mount St. Michael, and only a few brave fishermen had dared to try their luck and brave the Celtic Sea.

On the second day, I happened to see a single boat making the trip to the island. From my vantage point, it looked a great deal like the boat I had hired, but with the rain pouring down, it was impossible to say with any great degree of certainty.

Finally, on the third day, the rain subsided considerably although it was still drizzling. However, by early afternoon a weak sun finally made an appearance and everything seemed brighter and calmer.

I had spent most of the time working on my notes and considering the possibility of really writing a historical novel set in Cornwall. Green had sulked about the hotel – anxious to be doing I knew not what.

That morning after breakfast, Green said, "How much longer must we wait here for Holmes?"

"I have no idea," I replied, "but he asked us to stay here and do nothing until his return, and Holmes never makes requests lightly. There is always a method to his seeming madness. Consider, he has broken the code, he discovered the message in the Temple Church and he has led us here. I, for one, have faith in Holmes and his methods. I would suggest, despite your impatience, you do the same."

Green looked suitably chastised, and finally said, "Shall we go down to the beach and examine the causeway? I believe the tides are with us at present."

With nothing else to do and plenty of free time, I agreed, and some twenty minutes later we found ourselves at the beginning of the causeway that led to Mount St. Michael. Made of irregularly sized cobblestones worn smooth by time and the sea, the walkway was straight for the most part but out near the island there was an obvious curve that was visible from the mainland. I supposed it had something to do with protecting the jetty and at the same time creating a protected harbor on the shoreline.

As we stood there gazing at the island, Green asked me, "Do you think the treasure might be out there, and if so, how on Earth will we find it?"

I paused a moment before answering. I recalled that Holmes had met me alone and that was by design. Although he had not expressly cautioned me against sharing what little I knew with Green, neither had he encouraged it.

"I wish I could answer you, Captain, but truth be told, we still cannot say for certain whether the treasure even exists. Perhaps it was captured by bandits, perhaps some minion of the king at that time was able to secure it and 'neglected' to mention it to the Crown. As for how to find it if it is there, I'm going to put my faith in Sherlock Holmes. You do not know him as I do, so you cannot fully appreciate the gifts he possesses."

The answers seemed to satisfy Green, for he replied, "You are correct, Doctor. I know I certainly would have never thought to inspect the church window, nor do I know how he did it, but Holmes did crack the code. So we will bide our souls in patience until we are called to action."

Looking at him, I couldn't fully appreciate everything he had endured to arrive at this point. From somewhere in the back of my brain, I managed to summon up the last line from the sonnet "On His Blindness" by John Milton.

"Remember," I said, "They also serve who only stand and wait.'"

After strolling along the beach for an hour or so, we returned to the hotel and just in time, it seems. The clouds had rolled back in and for the next two days it rained continuously. Finally, on the third day I awoke to find bright sun streaming through my windows, and when I descended to the dining room, I was greeted by Holmes who was sitting at one of the tables with Captain Green. Although they were both enjoying coffee, it was obvious they had waited for me before ordering breakfast.

Over scrambled eggs, beans, tomatoes and rashers of bacon, Holmes filled us in on his recent adventures. Then turning to Green, he inquired, "Have you ever heard of Sir Douglas of Deering?"

"I believe he was a member of the Knights Templar with connections to Edward II, but beyond that I cannot provide any additional information.

"Actually, Sir Douglas was a favourite of His Majesty, who named him Duke of Cornwall. Arrogant and haughty, Sir Douglas was expelled from England on more than one occasion, but King Edward always found a way to facilitate his return.

"How about Sir Geoffrey de Fortis?" continued Holmes. "Does that name ring a bell?"

"I know he too was a member of the order, but again, I cannot provide you with details."

"Sir Geoffrey was a protégé of **William de la More, the grand commander of the Templars in England,** As you know, William died in the Tower where Edward II had had him imprisoned. Geoffrey became the commander of the Templars in Hertfordshire. One of the last communiqués William dispatched was to Geoffrey and Geoffrey then abandoned his base to head south, stopping at Temple Church and then presumably heading to Mount St. Michael."

"Why would Sir Geoffrey abandon his post?"

"Presumably because Sir Douglas had been sent to relieve Sir Geoffrey of the treasure and deliver it to King Edward."

"Why would Sir Douglas violate his vows and turn against his brothers?" I asked.

"I can imagine that seeing his fellow knights arrested and imprisoned and being offered a sizable piece of Templar property, and quite possibly more, might have proved inducement enough for him to renounce his former comrades and switch sides."

Green looked at Holmes and said, "If I may, how did you come by these names, this information? I have been researching the Templars for years, and yet in a short time you appear to have learned more about their inner workings than I thought possible."

"For centuries the records of Edward II, along with various other important documents were stored in Winchester. Then from the 1740s onwards, they were moved, together with other Exchequer records, to the chapter house of Westminster Abbey. Finally, in 1859, they were transferred to the new Public Records Office in London. It took a great deal of painstaking research which is why I was gone so long, but I finally discovered the report of Sir Douglas of Deering to King Edward."

"And what made you think such records still existed?" asked Green.

"To begin with, we still have the Domesday Book, which dates from 1086, so the existence of such records was within the realm of possibility. However, even more important were the Templars themselves. In addition to being warriors, these knights were also bankers and businessmen. As such, there had to be records, it was just a question of determining whether they still existed – and if they did, locating them. I had a great deal of help from a number of different people."

"So what happened next?" I asked.

Holmes then briefly reiterated Deering's pursuit of Geoffrey, his being repulsed from the island on his nighttime foray and attempt to take Sir Geoffrey by surprise and his sailing to the island two days later only to discover it deserted. "However, in his report, Deering did make mention of finding the remains of a catapult on the island along with several coins and a few precious stones. It was his belief that Sir Geoffrey and his men had used the instrument to launch the coins and gems far out into the sea."

"What a remarkable tale!" I exclaimed.

"And Sir Geoffrey, what became of him?" asked Green.

"To the best of my knowledge, neither Sir Geoffrey nor any of his men were ever heard from again. Whether they were lost at sea, emigrated to another country and changed their names, no one can say for sure."

"So then the treasure is gone?" Green inquired, "Or if not gone, exactly, then scattered across the bottom of the Celtic Sea."

"Although that certainly appears to be the case, one cannot say with absolute certainty. If Sir Geoffrey were clever enough to elude Sir Douglas and escape, it is certainly possible that he made some sort of arrangements for the safekeeping of the gold and gems."

"Do you have any reason for thinking that?"

"A man as resourceful as Sir Geoffrey, from what little I have been able to learn about him, would not willingly disobey his superiors. Unfortunately, we do not know what his final order from Sir William was, but I think it is safe to say he was entrusted with keeping the fortune from falling into the hands of Sir Douglas and by extension King Edward.

"Now, he might have well have consigned it to a watery grave using a catapult to make certain it was launched deep into the briny depths, but I think it just as likely that he concealed the treasure somewhere on that island with the intention of retrieving it when conditions for the Templars improved."

"But they never did," I added. "At the beginning of this case, I remember you saying that the Templar lands and wealth were handed over to the Knights Hospitaller."

"As indeed they were, but many Templars defied the pope. Even some monarchs challenged the pontiff. In Portugal, King Denis I, refused to pursue and persecute the former knights. With his blessing the Templars simply changed their name, from 'Knights Templar' to the reconstituted 'Order of Christ.' There was also a parallel Supreme Order of Christ of the Holy See. Both were regarded as legitimate successors to the Knights Templar."

"So do they still exist in Portugal?" I asked.

"As a matter of fact, they do – but purely in a ceremonial sense," Holmes replied. "Over the centuries, their power continued to wan; as a result, the few knights who remain have been relegated to largely ceremonial roles within the government."

I asked, "Are there Knights Templar in other countries?"

"There are indeed, and that's where things get very interesting," said Holmes.

He then pulled a notebook from his pocket and proceeded to read from it. Before he began, he prefaced his remarks, "As you can imagine I have been researching the Templars and everything related to them in great detail.

Then turning back to his notes he ban, "Prior to his execution, de Molay invested one Jean-Marc Larmenius with his powers. As a result, Larmenius was recognised as Grand Master following de Molay's death. Over the next decade, it appears, he gathered together members – the remnants of the order who had gone underground – and in 1324 he issued the Order the Charter of Transmission, which remains one of the governing documents of the present-day order.

"Over the next few centuries, the Order operated in secret with an uninterrupted line of Grand Masters which continued until 1705. In March of that year a number of French nobles convened at Versailles. They elected Phillip, Duke of Orleans and later Regent of France for King Louis XV, as the Order's 41st Grand Master. In his dual roles as regent and Grand Master, he provided an official renewal and legitimisation of the Order of the Temple as a secular order of chivalry with its right to resume the use of the word sovereign in its title."

"So they still exist," said Green. "I knew it."

Holmes continued as if he had not been interrupted. "From Louix XV, we can trace a semi-direct line – Napoleon, as you know, rather got in the way on two different occasions – to Louis XVIII, who we know visited the cave at Royston. Did he know something? Suspect something? Was he looking for a clue? Who can say? But as you are both aware, I do not believe in coincidences.

"Given the tumultuous history of the French monarchy, with its exiles and many claimants – my favourite being Louis XIX whose reign lasted some 20 minutes, but I digress – it's no great stretch to imagine records and documents being handed down in secret only to be concealed or misplaced and then being rediscovered years, decades or even centuries later."

"So if I'm not misunderstanding you, the men who have been our adversaries, to use your term, are the latest generation of Knights Templar hailing from France?" asked Green.

"At the moment, that's how I read it," said Holmes, "although I have serious doubts about their French lineage. As you know the royal houses of England and France have been close on any number of occasions throughout history. So I will need more data before I can make a pronouncement with any degree of certainty. Another possibility is that these men may also be an underground order of the Templars here in England."

"So what is our plan going forward?" I inquired.

Holmes then proceeded to outline what sounded on the surface to be a bold course of action, intended to bring our foes to justice.

He finished by looking at Green and me and saying, "I will not try to deceive you. There is a definite element of danger should we choose to follow this path."

"I should think a sniper in Hyde Park and brigands on horseback have already posed a certain obvious risk," I said.

"Given what they have done to my home, I think we must follow the plan you have suggested. This thing must be resolved, and to my way of thinking, sooner is certainly better than later or, God forbid, not at all."

"Bravo, gentlemen. I congratulate you," said Holmes.

"Now, since we are agreed, I will set certain things in motion, but it may take a few more days to have all the disparate elements in place as well attempting to arrange those few variables that we can control."

After we had discussed things further, Holmes sent Green to the local post office with a few specific tasks. After he left us, I looked at Holmes and asked, "Was there really a French monarch who ruled for 20 minutes or did you make that up?"

Holmes looked at me with an expression of mock horror on his face and said, "To what end?" He then proceeded to relate the unfortunate details of the short-lived reign of Louis XIX.

I wasn't quite certain why Holmes had singled out that seemingly hapless monarch, but I knew that he never did anything without a reason.

Chapter 21

After we had talked, Holmes excused himself saying he had a few matters to which he had to attend as well as several telegraphs to send. When we parted, he was headed towards the beach while I decided to take a stroll through the charming village – a pleasure I had been denying myself until now.

After I reached the beach, I went looking for my boatman to tell him I would probably be requiring his services over the next few days. When I reached the pier, I saw that the place where he usually tied up his boat was empty. Looking toward the island, I thought I could pick out his sail but I couldn't say with certainty that it was he.

As it was still morning, I headed for the village of Marazion. Given the age of the village, which claims to be the oldest settlement in Cornwall, I was rather surprised that there were no historic buildings of note. The center of activity this morning seemed to be the railroad station. Marazion was served by the West Cornwall Railway, and it seemed there were a great many perishable goods – fish, fruit and vegetables – from the surrounding farms and harbours being loaded for the short trip to Penzance whence they would be carried to other parts of the country by faster trains.

I was just about to return to the hotel when the passenger train pulled in. As I watched the workers unload the mail car, I also saw three men descend from the single passenger car. I thought the stature of one looked terribly familiar. Before they could see me, I took a seat on a bench and buried my head in the travel guide I had purchased. As they walked by, I heard a familiar voice say, "… but we still don't know where Holmes is. It is imperative that we find him. After all, we cannot…" and then they faded out of earshot.

As unobtrusively as possible, I watched as they headed for the bay. Although I was tempted to follow them, I was afraid of being spotted. So I decided to go directly to the hotel and inform Holmes of what I had learned. It was only after I had checked the dining room and made inquiries after my friend that I realized: I didn't know where Holmes was either.

After an afternoon of fruitless pacing and intervals of searching for Holmes, I finally encountered my friend in the dining room when I went down for supper. As we had agreed to meet at half seven, I waited for Green to join us so I wouldn't have to repeat myself. I told Holmes and Green all about my excursion to town and my visit to the train station. When I told him about the men I had seen, Holmes seemed more pleased than surprised.

"So they have arrived in Marazion already. I knew they were nearby, but truthfully, I hadn't expected them here for another day or two."

"Perhaps they are just reconnoitering?" I suggested.

"Perhaps," replied Holmes. "In fact, I think that is an altogether likely explanation for their presence here."

"Why do you say that?"

"Coming here as they did, they chanced being seen – as indeed they were – so obviously that risk now must seem minimal compared to whatever gain they think they stand to make."

"Why were you expecting them?" I exclaimed.

"Because we are moving inexorably to the denouement of this tortured tale, and I, for one, am more than ready to leave this business behind us and move onto something a bit more stimulating."

I thought to myself that except for those days when the rain had kept me indoors this case had been plenty invigorating, but I decided to hold my tongue.

"So now that they are here, do you have an immediate plan of action?"

Gazing toward the island, Holmes said, "I need at least two more days to put everything in place, so it is imperative that you and Captain Green remain safe. The worst thing that could happen would be for them to capture one or both of you and use that as leverage against me."

I promised Holmes I would remain either in my room or on the grounds of the hotel for the next two days. Green also swore that he would take no chances and would confine himself to the hotel grounds.

After we had finished our meal and smoked a cigar on the veranda, Holmes walked off into the night, departing in his usual enigmatic fashion. As he left, he would say only, "I have several important tasks to which I must attend."

And so it was that that Captain Green and I, having promised Holmes that safety would be our paramount concern, found ourselves limited to the hotel grounds for the next two days with little to occupy our time or minds.

The following morning, I breakfasted alone and found myself reading *The Times* as I enjoyed a second and then a third cup of coffee. Green had opted to sleep in. Had I followed my normal routine, I might have missed it entirely, but as I was already bored, I read the paper from front page to last, skipping nothing.

There it was – a small article which I had nearly overlooked. It was tucked away in a roundup of local crimes in London and as I read the paper, I was wishing that Holmes were with me. For I am certain this bit of news would have piqued his curiosity, for it certainly caught my attention. The pertinent piece was topped with a subhead that read: Inner Temple library burgled.

Although the details were sketchy, it appeared that a seldom-used section of the library, dating from its founding during the reign of King Henry II in the 12th century, had been broken into and burgled sometime within the past two months. The theft had been discovered only because a land dispute between two rival noblemen had led the parties to research ancient property lines and title grants. No one could remember the last time anyone had expressed a need to examine such records so it was impossible to say when the theft had occurred or what exactly had been taken.

I wondered what Holmes would make of the theft. Surely it didn't require any great leap of faith or imagination to see that whatever documents had been stolen must in some way be connected with our present endeavours. I thought about mentioning it to Green but then decided against it.

The rest of the day was spent largely indoors, reading and writing. The next morning, I scoured the papers for a follow-up story but could find nothing. I took a short walk around the grounds of the hotel, and when I returned I found Holmes at the front desk where he was checking in.

"And how long will you be staying with us, sir?" the clerk asked.

"That's difficult to say," replied Holmes. "Certainly tonight and tomorrow night as well I should think, but whether I shall require a third night here, I cannot say at this moment."

"Fortunately, things have slowed down a bit, so we should be able to accommodate any last-minute decisions on your part, Mr. Holmes."

Holmes thanked the young man and turning, he spotted me. "Doctor, I was wondering where you might have got to. All is well, I hope. And where is Captain Green.?"

"I am well, Holmes. I see you have checked in under your own name."

"Yes, there's no longer any need for an alias. They know where we are, and so far things are proceeding just as I might have hoped."

"Really?" I inquired with just a hint of sarcasm in my voice.

"Indeed," said Holmes, ignoring my barb. Since he proffered no explanation, I decided not to pursue the matter.

We then spent some time catching up, and when I mentioned the burglary at the Temple Library, he merely replied, "So you noticed that, too, did you? I don't know exactly what they might have learned, but it has certainly spurred them on."

We then moved onto other topics before heading to our rooms to prepare for dinner.

That night the three of us dined together, and Holmes outlined the plans for tomorrow. "I should like to get to the island around two or three in the afternoon," he began.

"But what about sunlight?" asked Green. "If we are there for any length of time, we could easily find ourselves working in the darkness."

"I think that is the least of our concerns. Now you both have Gladstones? If I am correct we may well need them to transport the treasure down to the shore."

"Do you really believe the treasure is on the island?" Green continued, "And if it is, are you certain you can locate it?"

"Certain? No," replied Holmes, "but if it is there, I am reasonably sure that I have ascertained its location."

Holmes then continued outlining the plan, but without his usual specificity which I found rather surprising.

When we headed for our rooms later, I said, "You seemed rather chary with the details of your scheme. I do hope that you have allowed for unforeseen contingencies."

"You noticed that, did you? Well-done, Watson!" said Holmes, and with that he entered his room, saying nothing further.

At breakfast the next morning, Holmes was conspicuous by his absence. When he failed to appear at lunch, I began to have some slight misgivings. As I ate, I kept an eye on the darkening sky.

However, my apprehension about Holmes vanished when there was a knock on my door at a quarter to two, and I heard Holmes say, "It's getting near time. I'll see you downstairs at three."

After cleaning up, I went down and met Holmes and Green in the lobby. When we stepped outside, I saw that it had begun to drizzle and the sun showed no signs of returning.

I looked at Holmes and asked, "Are you sure you want to do this in weather that could turn into a downpour at any moment?'

"Absolutely!" he exclaimed. "I welcome the rain – especially today."

As you might expect I was thoroughly confused by that statement and when Green looked at me, all I could do was shrug my shoulders.

Holmes then looked at us and said, "Good, you have your bags. The shovels and spade are there against the wall." While Green and I grabbed shovels, Holmes took up the spade. The three of us then walked to the beach. I started to turn towards the boats, but Holmes said, "Given that the tide is with us, I'd prefer to use the causeway to get to the island. Any of the sailors here are certain to remember three men with bags and shovels heading to the island."

I am sure anyone who might have seen us walking towards Mount St. Michael might have been struck by the odd sight of three men carrying bags and shovels but no umbrellas walking in the ever-increasing rain. Perhaps fifteen minutes later, we stepped onto the island and ten minutes after that we stood by the Mount St. Michael's Cross. I had little desire to return to that high ledge but I kept my discomfort to myself.

Holmes walked right up to the cross and said, "As I've often told you, Watson, you see but you do not observe."

"I examined that cross thoroughly," I protested. "I found nothing."

"Is there something there?" Green asked excitedly.

"Indeed, there is," replied Holmes. "Come, take a look." So saying, he opened his Gladstone and withdrew a dark lamp. After lighting it – no small feat in the rain – he knelt down next to the cross and covering the lamp with his Inverness, shone it upward so it illuminated the underside of the left arm of the crossbar. Although they were faint, there were obvious symbols carved into the stone. When I looked at the underneath of the right side, I saw that it was blank and smooth.

"My word, Holmes! How on Earth did you discover them and how did you know to look on this cross."

"A little research revealed that the other three crosses are relative newcomers to the island. In fact two were placed here in this century. This is the only cross that stands *in situ* and therefore it was the only cross that might have been here when Sir Geoffrey and his men arrived on the island."

"Bravo, Mr. Holmes. That is wonderful," exclaimed Green, who had taken the lantern and was now examining the symbols. "They are very faint and barely discernable.

Have you any idea what they translate to, or must we copy them down and try to solve the code ourselves?"

"No need for long hours of study this time," replied Holmes. "They are written in Latin."

"Oh, I saw what I thought was an 'X' first and assumed it was the Templar symbol for 'N.'"

"You are correct about the 'X' but it is also the Roman numeral 10. I have made a tracing and the letters read '*x gradus relicto.*'"

"Ten steps left," exclaimed Green. "Are you sure?"

"I am certain that's what the letters say, but as for whether the treasure is there, well, there is but one way to find out."

Holmes then proceeded to walk ten paces away from the left side of the cross. Turning back to us, he said, "I think we should start here."

Holmes then took the spade and made the outline of a hole about three feet wide by five feet long. Green and I then began to dig. Due to the rain the earth was quite soft at first, and we had dug a foot down in a very short while.

"If the treasure is here, we have no idea what it may be contained in," said Green, "so I would suggest that we take very shallow shovelfuls of earth from this point on. Whatever container it may be in, we don't want to damage it."

At that point, Holmes took the shovel from me and he and Green continued to dig. As you might expect the work now went much more slowly and every five or ten minutes the one without the shovel would relieve one of the diggers.

I had just taken the shovel from Green and thrust it into the dirt perhaps an inch or two when I felt a resistance that seemed unusual. "I may have struck something," I said.

Immediately, Green said, "Then we should start digging by hand."

As Holmes had suggested, we were all wearing rather disreputable clothing and had all brought gloves. I dropped to my knees and began scooping handfuls of dirt out of the hole. For his part Green did the same at the other end of the excavation. At one point, I gazed up to find Holmes peering intently into the hole with those hawk-like eyes. With the rain in my face, it may have been my imagination, but I thought I saw him smile and give an almost imperceptible nod of the head.

After the fifth or sixth handful, I saw something dark that was quite a different hue from the earth surrounding it. "I see something," I exclaimed. Gently digging around, I soon saw that it was some sort of ceramic container. It was cracked in places but in one piece as far as I could see. I kept digging on one side while Green had joined me and was pulling away dirt from the other.

Eventually, we lifted a large pot from the ground. I looked around, and Holmes said, "You found it, Watson, so please do the honors." I then looked at Green who also nodded. The lid was stuck having been held in place by the dirt for years, perhaps centuries. With the aid of my pocketknife, I was finally able to pry one side of it up and then I lifted it off.

The pot was filled with gems of all colors and sizes. There were also a number of pieces of jewelry – rings, bracelets, chains – all encrusted with precious stones.

"My word," I exclaimed, "this may rival even the Agra Treasure, now at the bottom of the Thames." Looking around, I asked, "Do you think there's more?"

"There's only one way to find out," Green replied and he immediately began scooping more handfuls of dirt from the hole. Without the use of tools, it was slow and painstaking work but after another three hours, we had found two more pots – both of these were filled with gold coins.

As you might expect, the hole had grown both longer and wider – not to mention deeper – but after yet another hour passed without any further finds, Holmes said, "I think that we have found all there is to find. There may be more, and I am certain that others will want to excavate further but I think we have done all we can for today. We have lost the sun, so let us return to the hotel, secure what we have found and make plans to return tomorrow morning."

By this time we were all filthy, and the three of us were standing in a hole up to our waists.

"So what do we do next, Holmes?" I asked.

"I propose that after we transfer the coins and gems to the Gladstones, make our way back to the Godolphin Hotel for a proper bath with hot water and soap and then we celebrate with the best dinner money can buy," said Green.

We set about shifting the money into the bags and as we worked my mind was running in a dozen different directions. I had long ago forgot about the rain. That was in the past – I was now firmly focused on the future.

As you might expect, I was thrilled to discover that our labours had ended, and I could almost taste the warming whisky when my reverie was interrupted by a familiar voice that said, "I simply don't know how to thank you, gentlemen."

Chapter 22

The voice continued, "Not only have you found the treasure but you've also packed it as well."

I was stunned when I looked up and saw the man from the bridge in Hyde Park and another fellow standing about twenty feet away. They both held pistols aimed at us, and I could only look longingly in the direction of our coats, which both Green and I had doffed and pushed under a bush while digging. As you might expect, our pistols were in the pockets.

In a manner eerily reminiscent of Holmes, the man said, "Don't even think about trying for your sidearm, Doctor Watson. I don't want to hurt anyone, but having come this far and with the end in sight, I am fully prepared for bloodshed should it become necessary."

"You won't get away with this," Green shouted. "We found the treasure; it's ours."

"If you want to get technical," the man countered, "it actually belongs to the Crown. Fortunately, Her Majesty will never miss what she never had, and unless my legal studies were for naught, I'm inclined to believe that possession is nine-tenths of the law."

As he was speaking, his companion was carrying the bags from the side of the pit and placing them at the other fellow's feet. When he had finished, the man looked down and then back to us and said simply, "Now since I am in possession of the treasure, it's mine."

He then turned to his fellow thief and said, "I think it might be prudent to relieve Dr. Watson and Captain Green of their sidearms – just in case. The man then walked to where we had placed our coats beneath the bush and after rifling through the pockets, stuck my pistol as well as Green's in the pockets of his coat.

Holmes had remained oddly silent throughout this entire exchange, and the fellow with the pistol finally took notice of it. "Cat got your tongue, Mr. Holmes?"

"Not at all, Sir Adrien. In fact, I was rather hoping you and your companion would have arrived somewhat earlier and offered to help with the digging."

"Oh that's rich, Mr. Holmes. Although I must say that I know many who'd be more than happy to help you dig your own grave."

"If you are planning on shooting us, I'd advise against it," said Holmes rather coolly.

"And why is that, sir?" he countered.

"I learned a very valuable lesson from you at Hyde Park."

"And what, pray tell, would that be?"

"Always keep a shooter in reserve. Just as I am certain you have a sniper concealed somewhere with his rifle trained on us in the event anything should go awry, so too, do I have a rifleman hidden, and he will put a bullet through your heart should you endanger our lives."

"You're bluffing," Sir Adrien said.

"Am I?" asked Holmes innocently. "There's but one way to find out. You may be able to kill one of us – although from that distance with a handgun you're far more likely to wound – and that's the only shot you or your friend will get off.

"There is a bright side to all this," continued Holmes.

"Oh?" said Sir Adrien.

"Indeed, if you fire at us my shooter will drop the both of you and then this hole won't go to waste and you can buried where the treasure you so desperately sought has resided for centuries."

That thought seemed to give the man pause. After a moment, he said, "It appears that we have reached something of an impasse. Here's what I suggest: You remain standing in the pit for twenty minutes while my associate and I leave with the treasure. I'll tell my man to stand down after that time and then everyone emerges from this situation safe and unharmed."

"You have to leave half the treasure," said Green.

"Do I?" said Sir Adrien. "I thought we had covered the concept of possession and the law earlier. No, Captain Green, I'm afraid the booty leaves with me and in return, you leave here with your lives. Is that acceptable, Mr. Holmes?"

"You really haven't given me much of a choice," replied Holmes.

"Remain where you are for twenty minutes while my friend and I depart. You won't know how long my sniper has remained in position but if he sees you move before the allotted time, he will shoot you. Having said that, let me wish you a good day, gentlemen. And again, let me thank you for your labours, both with regard to discovering the location and then excavating and packing the treasure for us."

As he spoke he and his companion were backing up the hill towards the castle. While his associate lugged two of the bags, Sir Adrien carried the third and his pistol never wavered as he covered us. Although I thought it highly unlikely that he could hit any of us from that distance, I was cognizant of the possibility of an unseen sniper lurking nearby.

After they had crested the hill, I turned to Holmes, who had lit a cigarette and was the picture of serenity, and said, "What should we do?"

Glancing at his watch, he said, "I'd strongly suggest that we wait for eighteen more minutes and then make our way back to the mainland."

After another five or six minutes had passed, Green exclaimed, "I've had enough of this. While we stand here doing nothing, they're getting away with the treasure."

"We have but twelve more minutes to wait," replied Holmes evenly.

"You can't be serious," exclaimed Green.

Having said that he moved to climb out of the hole, but Holmes grabbed his arm and pulled him back in. "Although I do not have a sniper positioned in the bushes, there is little doubt in my mind that Sir Adrien does. If you are shot and killed, you will never recover the treasure. If we wait just a few more minutes, we may be able to track them and bring them to justice in the future."

"And if they should get away clean?"

"No one gets away from Sherlock Holmes unless Holmees wishes it," I said, defending my friend's decision, even though deep inside I was more disposed to take Green's side.

Glancing around at the trees in the distance, Green suddenly appeared to realize the narrow escape he had just had. "I suppose you are right, Mr. Holmes, but just to stand here and watch them walk away is positively maddening."

"Believe me, Captain Green, I share your exasperation. However, in this case I am certain that discretion is the better part of valour."

Suddenly it hit me, "Holmes, how are we going to get back to the mainland? I would assume that by now the tides are against us, and the boatmen have all retired for the night. Sir Adrien and his friends obviously arrived by boat so they have transportation to the mainland waiting. However, the decision to use the causeway this morning may mean that we end up spending the night on this blasted rock."

"I am sure we can borrow a boat from the St. Aubyn family, and if that we fails, perhaps we can signal the mainland from the shore," offered Green.

"Not to worry, gentlemen," said Holmes, "I promise you that we will be back on shore," and he paused to glance at his watch, "within the hour."

I looked at Holmes and wondered how we were going to get to the mainland – much less catch up with the thieves. After glancing at his watch one more time, he climbed out of the hole and extended a hand to me as Green was pulling himself out. When we were all on equal footing and had donned our sodden coats, he simply said, "Follow me," and began to walk away from the castle towards the sea.

"You're going the wrong way," Green said.

"Am I? I think not," Holmes replied and continued with a determined stride toward the rear of the island and away from the village of Marazion. At one point, we started down a steep path towards the beach and when we reached the bottom, Holmes turned to his right and began walking towards the end of the beach. When we reached the base of the cliff, he reached down and pulled back a tarpaulin. Underneath was a small rowboat. We dragged it to the surf and got in.

I was taken aback when Green grasped the oars. Seeing the surprise on my face, he looked at me, smiled and said, "I was a Blue on the Cambridge rowing team."

He began to pull on the oars and it was immediately obvious that he was an experienced rower. I knew Holmes was an athlete of sorts and wondered if he might give Green a run for his money. However, when I looked over at my friend, I was struck by the expression of equanimity on his face.

Then it hit me, "Holmes, how did you know that a boat would be there?"

"Because I placed it there."

"Of course you did! But when? Why?"

"I visited Mount St. Michael before you had even arrived in the village, my friend. As I had expressed to you when we first discussed this place, there is always the danger of being cut off, so I took steps to make certain that couldn't happen."

Green was pulling hard and a moment later we rounded the western tip of the island, and I could see the lights of the village in the distance. I was surprised when Holmes said to Green, "Would you like me to take over?"

"No, thank you Mr. Holmes. This is nothing compared to a good day on the Cam, something I've missed sorely since my days at university."

Some fifteen minutes later, we pulled up to the small jetty. It was twilight and there was no one around. "Where to now, Holmes?"

"I think our best bet is to visit the chief of the local constabulary," he replied so we then set out for Fore Street. As we walked past the hotel, I could only look longingly at the window of my room as I thought about hot water and soap to be followed by a delicious dinner and several glasses of whisky neat.

Finally, we reached a small building that was obviously somebody's house. Holmes knocked on the door and a older woman answered. After introducing himself, the woman said, "We've been expecting you, Mr. Holmes. Bill is out in the barn with the others. It's just around back."

We walked to the back of the house where we saw a sturdy but well-weathered barn. Two men were standing outside the door and they merely nodded at Holmes, Green and myself without saying a word. I assumed they were locals whom "Bill," whoever he might be, had summoned. When Holmes knocked on the door, a voice from inside said, "Come in, Mr. Holmes. We've been awaiting your arrival."

Holmes pulled open the door and stepped inside. Green followed, and I brought up the rear. I was stunned to see Inspectors Gregson and Lestrade, both holding rifles, standing guard over three men who lay trussed up on the floor like so many sacks of grain.

I was even more surprised to see the old boatman who had ferried me back and forth to Mount St. Michael standing there, also holding a rifle.

Before anyone could say anything, he looked at us and exclaimed "Aree faa! What have you fellas been up to?"

What followed was a cacophony of questions and observations as well as one or two jibes by the Scotland Yard inspectors. To say I was puzzled would be an understatement of gargantuan proportions. Finally, Holmes held his hands up and said, "Let's have some sort of order, shall we?"

After things had quieted, he began by saying, "Gregson, Lestrade, thank you for acting so promptly. Can I assume our friends here offered little resistance?"

"We were waiting for them at the jetty," Gregson replied. "When we saw the three Gladstones, we knew these were our men. Once they had their hands full, we put the rifles on them and they pretty much gave up."

"I think that one," said Lestrade, pointing to one of Sir Adrien's companions, "had a thought or two about reaching for his rifle. But a neatly placed shot by Gregson soon drove that thought from his head."

Looking at the man Lestrade had indicated. I suddenly realized that I had seen him several times before on the pier and once on the island. I had assumed that he was a local, so I decided to keep my recognition to myself.

Turning to the boatman, Holmes said, "I must also thank you Chief Thornton for your cooperation and willingness to go along."

"We may not be as sophisticated as you London folk, but your name is well-known in Cornwall, Mr. Holmes. Besides, I've been the law here for nearly thirty years, and outside of the Newlyn riots earlier this year, we've never had anything like this in Marazion."

I couldn't help myself, "The Newlyn riots? Pray tell what could have caused such unrest in such a bucolic locale?"

Thornton laughed. "As you know Cornwall is sometimes referred to as the land of saints. We are a religious lot, and as a result, the local fishermen refused to fish on Sunday, preferring instead to 'keep holy the Lord's day.' When other fleets got wind of that, they began to take advantage of the opportunity. Some of the boys took matters into their own hands and began to seize and board non-Cornish vessels, throwing their catch overboard. After three days of rioting, it was only the presence of a naval destroyer that brought things back to normal."

Having concluded his reminiscence, he continued, "Speaking of riots, the three of you look as though you just fought in one. I'm guessing you could do with a wee dram."

"I'm all for that!" I exclaimed, which gave everyone a chuckle. Thornton then left to fetch a bottle and glasses.

While he was gone, Lestrade took the measure of the three of us and said, "I've seen you in many different situations, Mr. Holmes, but I must say, I don't think I've ever seen you looking so … disheveled."

At that Gregson joined the conversation saying, "Why don't you just say it, Lestrade? They look like something the cat dragged in."

At that we all had a good chuckle, Holmes included. A moment later, Thornton was back with a bottle of whisky and six glasses. After he had poured "wee drams" for everyone, Green said, "A toast! To Mr. Sherlock Holmes and the treasure of the Templars."

Before we could raise our glasses, a voice from the floor proclaimed, "It doesn't belong to you, and I will be avenged." Sir Adrien then proceeded to revile us all with a stream of oaths and curses.

Having had enough, Chief Thornton said, "Another word from you and the gag goes in. I'm sure I've got some dirty rags here somewhere."

With that, the man lapsed into silence.

"You are quite correct," replied Holmes, looking down at Sir Adrien. "The treasure does not belong to us, but it doesn't belong to you either. I believe both the coins and gems are the property of the Crown and as for threats –

yours isn't the first and I am certain it will not be the last – yet here I stand."

With that, we all raised our glasses and exclaimed, "Hear! Hear!"

"Looks as though you've done it again, Mr. Holmes," said Lestrade.

Holmes looked at the inspector and replied, "I appreciate the sentiment, Inspector, but in this case I had a great deal of help, from the long-suffering Dr. Watson to the intrepid Captain Green, to both you and Inspector Gregson. However, this might have had a much different ending had I not encountered Chief Thornton. Believe me when I tell you that his assistance has proven invaluable."

With that we toasted Thornton, and after another few rounds, which the inspectors refused, Lestrade said, "Mr. Thornton, Inspector Gregson and I are officially relieving you of your prisoners in the name of the Crown. There's a train at half eight which we can take to Penzance and thence back to London."

As he was speaking, Gregson was helping the men off the floor. I saw that in addition to darbies on their wrists, they had been shackled at the ankles and they were all chained together. "The first bit of trouble from any of you, and you will rue the day," growled Gregson.

As Gregson led them out of the barn, Thornton yelled, "You'll mail back the chains and shackles?"

Lestrade laughed and reaching into his pocket, pulled out some notes and handing them to Thornton said, "It's probably easier all the way around if you just buy some new ones. I'm sure the Yard will reimburse me."

Then he began following the last prisoner out the door. Just as he reached it, he turned back and said, "I'll expect you'll fill me in on everything once you have returned to London, Mr. Holmes."

"You have my word, Inspector. You and Gregson can both come to Baker Street, and I'll ask Mrs. Hudson to make something special for dinner."

After they had departed, at Thornton's insistence we all shared one more "wee dram," and as we left for the hotel, Holmes thanked him and tried to push something into his palm. Although Thornton initially resisted, Holmes remained adamant saying, "You have more than earned this, my friend. What you do with it is up to you."

Thornton said, "Are you sure, Mr. Holmes?"

"I would not say, if I weren't. Now, I can see that Watson and Green are eager to wash up – as am I – so let me thank you again."

I added, "If you ever make it to London, you must promise me that you will visit us at Baker Street."

"Highly unlikely, Doctor. As I told you in the boat, I've never been more than ten miles from here, and I certainly don't intend to start now, but your invitation is most welcome."

After shaking hands all around, we headed back to the hotel. When we arrived, we all went to our rooms to clean up. After a thorough wash, I entered the dining room some forty minutes later where I saw Holmes sitting alone at a table.

I sat down, looked at him and said, "You could have told me about Thornton."

"I needed you to act naturally. As you now know, you were under constant surveillance and any suspicious glances on your part might have given away the game."

"Speaking of giving things away, if I may ask, what was it you were trying to give Thornton just before we left?"

"Nothing so terribly important – just one of the smaller diamonds from the treasure we recovered."

To say I was flabbergasted would not do me justice, but I tried to regain my composure as I spotted Green approaching the table. "We will talk more of this," I said.

"Of course," replied Holmes, who then turned and waved to Green.

Chapter 23

After the day we had endured, I'm pretty certain that even the humblest fare would have seemed like a grand feast. However, the hotel cooks outdid themselves and after we had eaten our fill and relaxed with cigars and brandies, Green said, "Mr. Holmes, if I may ask: How did you manage it?"

"Actually, once I made one or two discoveries, things rather fell into place of their own accord."

"Do tell," I encouraged him, for there were a number of things I wanted cleared up as well.

"As you might expect, my suspicions were aroused when we were visited by a woman claiming to be your late daughter. I remember telling Watson at the time that it was obvious someone either wanted us in Royston very badly or else out of London.

"As it turns out, it was a combination of both. They wanted us to examine the cave at Royston to see if we could discover anything they might have missed. They also wanted us out of London, so they could search the flat at Baker Street to ascertain whether we had made any progress on our own that we had not shared with the young lady.

"You may recall, Watson, that Mrs. Hudson informed us when we returned from Royston that a man had been in to check the gas. Although you complain about my untidiness, there is a definite method to the manner in which I store and arrange things. I had but to glance at my desk to tell it had been rifled."

"Really?" I asked with just a hint of sarcasm in my voice.

"Truly," replied Holmes earnestly. "Things were neatly stacked and arranged. I'm certain they thought I would attribute it to the housekeeper, but as you are well aware Mrs. Hudson and those in her employ who might enter our rooms have a strict prohibition against touching my papers."

"And yet you said nothing," I exclaimed.

"Again, I apologize, but your face is an open book. I wanted them to think their intrusion had gone unnoticed.

"My suspicions about our adversaries were further aroused when we met the bogus Captain Green in Hyde Park. Initially, Sir Adrien hoped to convince me to work with him, but when that failed he adopted an entirely different tack. If you recall, Watson, his first words to me were 'Now then, Mr. Holmes.'"

"Yes, I remember thinking there was something odd about his speech. And now that you mention it, when he stopped Captain Green and me on the road, he opened the conversation by saying 'Now then, Dr. Watson.' As soon as I heard the phrase used that way I was pretty certain it was the man from Hyde Park."

"Excellent!" Holmes exclaimed, "I keep saying we'll make a detective of you yet."

During this bit of back and forth, Green merely sat there with a confused look on his face."

"My apologies, Captain Green," said Holmes. "Please allow me to explain. While the words 'now then' in standard English are generally used to draw a person's attention to something, among Yorkshiremen, it's a common way of saying hello. That coupled with several other phrases – *bleedy* for bloody, *chelpin* for talking and *faffin* for fooling around – were dead giveaways. For the most part, he did an admirable job concealing his accent, but when we later received the letters signed 'Seneschal, Temple Yorkshire,' I wasn't terribly surprised.

"I also owe you an apology, Captain Green. There were actually three words carved into the frame surrounding the stained glass window in the church on the moor."

"So that's why you discouraged me from looking for myself?"

"Exactly."

"What was the third word, Holmes?" I inquired.

"Along the very top of the window, directly opposite the word *horae* was the word *arum*."

"Gold" exclaimed Green. "How could I have missed it?"

"Quite easily. You see you weren't looking for it, but I was."

"But why?"

"Because when people are reading or writing, they generally look down, as you did and as I did initially. However, leaving a secret message that you hope will be found requires an entirely different thought process. So I examined the entire frame which led me first to the *horae* followed shortly thereafter by the Templar symbols – and then I looked up. There at the very top of the frame was the word *arum*.

"Given what we know of the Templar who carved the symbols – it only made sense that there should be three words – denoting the Holy Trinity, their vows and who knows what else."

"So you then knew the treasure was to be found here."

"I wouldn't say 'knew' but I'll certainly grant you that I strongly suspected that the gold had at least been brought and quite possibly concealed here."

"Why do you think they separated the words so?" I asked.

"I can only guess that whoever left the message wanted to make it as clear as possible – under what I imagine were rather vexing circumstances. Whoever the writer was, he wanted clarity which is difficult to achieve in so brief and so vague a message. In short, he didn't want someone searching for a 'gold hour.' so he tried to indicate that although the words were connected they were not linguistically part of a single sentence."

"That's brilliant, Holmes!" I exclaimed.

And then as though it had just occurred to him, Captain Green looked around and said, "Mr. Holmes, what has become of the treasure?"

In all the excitement of the capture of Sir Adrien and his associates – and aided by the several wee drams imbibed in the barn – the fate of the Gladstones had slipped my mind as well. I recalled that they had left with Gregson, Lestrade, and the prisoners, but I hadn't given any thought to their ultimate destination.

"As we speak, I am certain that it is on a train from Penzance to London with several agents from Her Majesty's government keeping a watchful eye on it."

Since Holmes had remained calm, I suspected that I knew how that had been arranged. As a result I held my tongue. I wasn't surprised when Holmes said, "My friend in the government – the one who arranged the special train for us – sent along four armed men to accompany Lestrade and Gregson. I believe you saw two of them standing outside Thornton's barn when we arrived. I should imagine the presence of those men on the beach played no small role in convincing Sir Adrien and his associates to surrender without a struggle."

"That's all well and good" replied Green, "and while I am glad that Her Majesty's government has taken charge of it, do you have any idea what is to become of it in the future?"

"I cannot say for certain," replied my friend, "but I have little doubt that when we return to London, some sort of arrangement can be arrived at which will prove satisfactory to all parties."

"I should hope so," said Green, who appeared mollified, if not totally convinced. At any rate, he decided not to press the issue further.

"But how did you tumble to Sir Adrien?" I asked. "How did you learn that name? And how was he able to discover the location of the treasure and then follow us undetected?"

"Let me take that in sections, starting with the last question and working backwards," replied Holmes. "I was always aware we were under observation. Although initially I didn't know by whom, I was constantly on the lookout for unfamiliar faces showing up repeatedly in different locations.

"As for how Sir Adrien became aware of the treasure that I cannot say with certainty."

"Can you not even hazard a gu— a supposition?" inquired Green, correcting himself with a chuckle.

Holmes looked at me and smiled, then he turned to Green and said, "I am glad to see that you remembered. I suppose in this case, I might be persuaded to share a theory I had developed at the time."

I had to struggle to contain my merriment. Despite all his fine words and pronouncements to the contrary, I knew Sherlock Holmes guessed all the time – although he would never call it that. How often had he heard an account of a case and formulated a theory before he had even arrived at the scene of the crime? However, knowing his flair for the dramatic, I held my tongue and let him tell his story in his preferred manner.

"Recently, the oldest section of the law library at Inner Temple was broken into, and a number of documents were taken. Since that particular section is not open to the general public, I can only surmise that one of Sir Adrien's associates stumbled across something he believed to be of significance. He obviously passed along the information to Sir Adrien and thus started a chain of events that was brought to my attention because some tallow droppings were found on the floor of the **Wallace Collection**.

"The law library was the beginning. Whatever they discovered there was what put them on the trail of the treasure. The visits to the Wallace Collection were the work of a professional thief. They were much neater and were it not for the bits of wax, they might have gone undetected."

"Well, if Sir Adrien oversaw these events, who actually carried them out?" asked Green.

"That I cannot say," replied Holmes. "Nor will I even hazard a theory or as you might call it a *guess*," he continued, emphasizing the last word.

I am not certain, but I think Green must have blushed, for Holmes smirked at his discomfort.

Then he relented and said, "They may have hired a professional and given him very specific instructions or perhaps there was a member of the Order who already possessed the requisite skills."

"When you say the Order, you don't mean..." and I let my voice trail off.

"I am afraid I do," he replied. Then looking about and seeing our glasses were empty, he said, "Would anyone care for one more 'wee dram' before we call it a night?"

When the drinks had arrived, Holmes, did something rather unusual for him. He looked at us and said, "I'd like to propose a toast to Templars past, present and future. May they always remember their motto: '*Non nobis Domine non nobis se Nomini Tuo da gloriam.*'"

When I looked at him quizzically, he translated, "Not to us, O Lord, not unto us, but to thy name give the glory."

To which Green and I both replied, "Amen."

Epilogue

When we returned to London, Holmes was as good as his word and over a delightful dinner prepared by Mrs. Hudson, he explained everything to Gregson and Lestrade as well as Smith, the historian; and Miss Falcetta, the linguist. As you might expect, Captain Green also attended.

Several weeks later, we learned that Sir Adrien and his companions were tried and convicted of armed robbery and an array of other charges. Although Sir Adrien demanded a trial by his peers in the House of Lords, a quick look into his title proved that it was patently false. He was the son of a Yorkshire carpenter who had purchased his title from a down-on-his-luck baronet. Once that was determined, he was tried as a commoner and sentenced to twenty years hard labour at Wandsworth Prison. His two associates were each sentenced to ten years.

The next few months passed rather quickly. Before I knew it the calendar had turned to September, and things had pretty much returned to normal. I was back at Barts, and, as you might expect, Holmes had moved on to other cases, not the least interesting of which was the one involving a dentist from Manchester, one Robert Griswold by name, who traveled down to London and went to Trafalgar Square where he constructed a wooden barrel, which he put together in full view of hundreds of passersby, having brought the pieces with him from Manchester. He then climbed inside, pulled on the top and was never seen again. However, that is a tale for another time.

I had slept in one morning after a particularly trying night at the hospital, and when I came down to breakfast,

Holmes was noticeably absent. By my place was a short note in his spidery hand leaning on my coffee cup:

Watson,

Any plans for this evening? If you have, liberate yourself. You should be aware libations begin at 7 p.m. I beseech you, abort any other engagements. If you can oblige me, I think you may well be eternally grateful. We depart at 6:45.

SH

My first thought was that it was the strangest note I had ever received from Holmes. In tenor and tone, it was most unlike him. As I read it over a second and third time, I found myself becoming a bit nettled by my friend's rather supercilious tone – "abort any other engagements" and "We depart at 6:45" indeed! Still, truth be told, I had no plans for the evening and my curiosity had definitely been piqued. I then turned my attention to the morning paper, looking as I always did, for anything that might arouse my friend's curiosity or appeal to his love of the outré. As was often the case, my search proved fruitless.

With little to occupy my time or my mind, the day seemed interminable. Finally, around half-five, I heard the front door open and close, followed a few minutes later by my friend's familiar tread as he ascended the stairs. Upon entering the room, he said, "Ah, I am glad you are here. I've asked Mrs. Hudson to prepare a light supper and then we can be on our way."

As he headed towards his room, he inquired, "Anything unusual in the papers today?"

When he returned a moment later, I replied, "No, nothing of note and certainly nothing that would interest you."

"I assume you have perused them in your usual meticulous manner?"

"I have," I replied. "Have I missed something important?"

"Perhaps," he replied enigmatically.

Deciding to change the topic, I asked, "Where exactly will we be on our way to later?"

"You know how you enjoy surprising your readers?"

"I have been known to engage in a literary flourish or two," I admitted.

"While you sometimes play fair and provide all the necessary clues, occasionally you have me arrive on the scene and function as a sort of *deus ex machina,* appearing at the end to have an apparent flash of genius and solve the mystery based on the depth to which the parsley had sunk in the butter on a hot day."

"Are you still upset about the way I depicted your handling of the Abernetty case?"

"What should have been a serious lesson in deduction has been romanticized by lurid sensationalism – but that's a discussion for another day." At that point, Mrs. Hudson knocked on the door and Holmes bade her enter.

Carrying a tray of various types of sandwiches and a pot of freshly brewed coffee, she said, "A light supper, as you requested, Mr. Holmes."

When we finished it was half six. Holmes sat back and taking stock of my appearance, said, "Might I suggest a fresh shirt and collar?"

"Where the deuce are we going, old man?"

"I've given you ample clues; it's up to you to divine the rest."

As I went up to my room to change, I kept turning over Holmes's words in my mind. Whatever clues he thought he had provided had certainly escaped my notice.

As I came back down, he was waiting for me at the door. After descending the stairs, we stepped out and there at the kerb was a hansom waiting for us. The carriage looked vaguely familiar but I was unable to recall where I had seen it before. The driver obviously knew our destination, for Holmes entered the cab without saying a word. As we drove along, my mind was whirling. The shades had been drawn so our destination remained a secret.

Eventually we stopped on Spanish Place – which I recognized only because I had frequented a tobacconist there – and entered a rather large building through the tradesmen's doorway. A young serving boy spotted us and ran ahead. It was only when we turned a corner and I saw "The Laughing Cavalier," hanging on the wall that I realized we were in the Wallace Collection.

We kept going forward through the semi-darkness until we turned a corner and brilliant light was spilling out of two open doors. As we neared I noticed a pair of pedestals – one on each side of the doorway. I stopped by the nearer one and was stunned when I read:

The Treasures of the Templars

An exhibition of coins and artifacts collected in England and hidden for centuries by the Knights Templar.

Curated by Captain Richard Green

With assistance from Sherlock Holmes and Dr. John Watson

As we entered the room, we were greeted by a spontaneous round of applause, initiated by Captain Green. Gazing around, I saw the faces of all those who had been involved in the case from the beginning. I saw Mr. Smith and Miss Falcetta as well as Miss Barbuto, Holmes's friend from the library. Looking further, I saw that even Mr. Pool and his wife had come down from Royston. To say I was overwhelmed would be an understatement.

As you might expect, there were speeches by Paul Rontondo, the head curator of the collection, as well as by Green.

Inside, the room seemed aglow from the reflection of the lights off the gold coins, Also, the individual jewels as well as those in the various pieces – bracelets, daggers, rings and a tiara – sparkled and shimmered as they caught the lights hitting them from various angles.

At one point, Green glanced at Holmes and me, and both of us shook our heads indicating we had no wish to address the crowd.

There was champagne and hors d'oeuvres and a great deal of small talk. Later in the evening, a woman approached Holmes and inquired if she might call upon him on the morrow. After a bit more discussion, he assented.

Finally, we left, and as it was an unseasonably warm late autumn night, we decided to walk to Baker Street. At one point, I said to Holmes, "I know you claim to have provided clues about this evening; it appears obvious I have missed them. What's even more puzzling is there was no announcement of this in the papers."

At that point Holmes began to laugh. "Watson, I will never get your measure. You have moments of stunning brilliance which, unfortunately, are offset by others of utter opaqueness.

"You said you read the papers?"

"I did."

"Carefully? From cover to cover? Did you read everything with your full focus or merely glance at the headlines?"

"Does it make a difference?"

"Indeed it does. For had you read carefully, you would have noticed that pages 5 and 6 as well as 15 and 16 had been taken from yesterday's paper to replace those same pages in the paper you read today."

Blushing, I said, "I assume the announcement of this opening was in today's paper."

"You assume correctly – page 5, the upper right hand corner, complete with a photograph."

"You said 'clues' I countered. That's only one."

"Have you the note I left for you?"

"No, it's on the table."

"When we return, glance down the page and you will notice that the first letter of each line spells out the word Wallace."

"My word, Holmes, that is clever. So once again, I have seen…"

"… but not observed," he said finishing my sentence for me.

At that we both chuckled, and at that point, in an effort to change the subject, "I asked, what did that woman you were speaking with want?"

"I cannot say for certain," he replied, "but if I heard her correctly, it involves a politician, a lighthouse and a trained cormorant."

"My word, what an odd assortment!"

"I should say, but I suppose we'll just have to wait until the morning to find out how they all tie together." He then lit a cigarette and paraphrased one of his favourite maxims, 'Life *really* is infinitely stranger than anything which the mind of man could invent ...'"

Author's Notes

There really is a Wallace Collection in London, featuring several rooms of armor. All the particulars regarding the building are accurate as far as I know. *The Laughing Cavalier* by Hals is a part of the collection, but to the best of my knowledge, the Collection has never possessed a shield that was owned by Jacques de Molay.

Speaking of de Molay, the history of the Knights Templar has become the stuff of legend, films, video games and a great deal of popular prose – both fiction and non-fiction. I have tried to present the Templars as honestly as I could. At one point, they may well have been the richest, most powerful organization in Europe.

As you might expect, hundreds of books have been written about them. If you are interested, you might want to investigate the *Knights Templar Encyclopedia: The Essential Guide to the People, Places, Events, and Symbols of the Order of the Temple* by Karen Ralls; *The Templars: The Rise and Spectacular Fall of God's Holy Warriors* by Dan Jones; and *The Knights Templar: A Captivating Guide to a Powerful Catholic Military Order and Their Impact on the Crusades* by Captivating History.

The Analytic Engine developed by Henry Babbage, which was the successor to his Difference Engine, is generally regarded as the precursor of today's modern computer. Although there was no Steven Imp who worked with him, the character of Lady Lovelace is a real person.

The daughter of Lord Byron and a brilliant mathematician, she is often regarded as the first computer programmer.

As I said, I have tried to be true to what is known about the Templars, but Sir Geoffrey and his men as well as Sir Douglas of Deering are all fictitious. The same may be said about the treasure, but as I pointed out in the book, anyone who keeps current with such things knows that new treasures are discovered on what seems to be a semi-regular basis. So just because we haven't learned of its existence yet doesn't mean that such a trove doesn't exist. Like so many other things, it may simply be waiting to be found.

All of the facts about the cave in Roystan are essentially true. Obviously, it was never visited by Holmes and Watson although the King Louis XVIII of France did indeed stop by while he was living in exile in England.

As for Cornwall, the Old Inn, the Godolphin Hotel, the village at Chysauster and the town of Marazion, they may all be visited today. The same is true of Mount St. Michael although I have taken a few liberties with the buildings on the island. To the best of my knowledge the four crosses mentioned are still standing and most of the details surrounding them are accurate.

Finally, if there are mistakes in this book, and I'm certain there are a few, the blame must be laid squarely at my feet. Sometimes no matter how many times you read something, you still manage to miss the obvious. So I apologize here for any errors you may discover.

Acknowledgments

I continue to maintain that writing, at least as I practice it, is a lonely task. You can't "Phone a Friend" and ask for a denouement or a plot twist, nor can you "Buy a Villain." Over the years, I've gotten into the habit of writing late at night when everyone else is in bed and the house is still. However, it has been made somewhat less onerous by the encouragement and patience of friends and family members, especially my wife, who have supported and cheered me on in my endeavors.

I should be terribly remiss if I failed to thank my publisher, Steve Emecz, who makes the process painless, and the enormously talented Brian Belanger, whose skill as a cover designer is unmatched. To have such talented friends is a blessing indeed.

No book is complete without a solid line edit, and Deborah Annakin Peters continues to provide that as well as a number of invaluable suggestions all of which have improved my books immeasurably. She also makes certain that my Britishisms are correct and that no Americanisms are allowed to creep in. My works are so much better because of her diligence and care.

I also owe a considerable debt to Dr. Robert Katz, a good friend, who remains the finest Sherlockian I know. He has continued to encourage me and is kind enough to read my efforts with an eye toward accuracy – both with regard to the Canon, and perhaps more importantly, to common sense.

To Francine and Richard Kitts, two outstanding Sherlockians, for their unflagging support and encouragement. Both of whom were kind enough to read the manuscript in its raw form and suggest improvements.

To my brother, Edward; and my sister, Arlene; who continue to believe in me even when I am constantly doubting myself.

I owe a special debt to many of my former students who have read and enjoyed my books and offered kind words of encouragement. You know who you are, and I can't thank you enough.

A special thanks to all those, and there are far too many to name, whose support for my earlier efforts have made me see just what a wonderful life I have and what great people I am surrounded by. So to all of you who have read my previous efforts, a sincere thank you.

To say that I am in the debt of all those mentioned here doesn't even begin to scratch the surface of my gratitude.

Finally, once again, if there are errors in this book – and I'm pretty sure there are – the only person responsible for them is me.

About the author

Richard T. Ryan is a native New Yorker, having been born and raised on Staten Island. He majored in English at St. Peter's College (now St. Peter's University) in Jersey City and pursued his graduate studies, concentrating on medieval literature, at the University of Notre Dame in Indiana.

After teaching high school and college for more than a decade, he joined the staff of the Staten Island Advance newspaper. He worked there for nearly 30 years, rising through the ranks to become news editor. When he retired in 2016, he held the position of publications manager for that paper although he still prefers the title, news editor.

In addition to his first novel, "The Vatican Cameos: A Sherlock Holmes Adventure," he has written "The Stone of Destiny: A Sherlock Holmes Adventure," "The Druid of Death," "The Merchant of Menace," "Through a Glass Starkly," "Three May Keep a Secret," "The Poisoned Pawn" and "The Devil's Disciples." Six of his novels have been published in Italian by Mondadori.

Other published works include "B Is for Baker Street: My First Sherlock Holmes Book," which he wrote for his grandchildren, Riley Grace and Henry Robert – and now Brody Edward. He has also penned three trivia books, including "The Official Sherlock Holmes Trivia Book."

Wearing a different hat, he serves as the editor for the *Year in Mystery* series for Belanger Books, which attempts to fill in the voids in the Sherlockian Canon. The first six books, 1881 through 1886, are available and the seventh and eighth volumes are due out later this year. Also for Belanger Books, he has co-edited *Writing Holmes,* a collection of essays on why and how people write about the world's Greatest Detective; and *Reading Holmes* as well as *Seeing Holmes,* due out sometime next year. He also served as editor for *No Holidays for Holmes,* a collection of short stories, and a second volume is expected sometime next year.

In a slightly different medium, he can also boast at having *Deadly Relations,* a mystery-thriller he wrote, produced off-Broadway on two separate occasions at the Playwrights Horizons Theatre.

And if that weren't enough, he is the very proud father of two children, Dr. Kaitlin Ryan-Smith and Michael Ryan, and the incredibly proud grandfather of the aforementioned Riley Grace and Henry Robert as well as Brody Edward, the newest member of the Ryan clan.

He has been married for 46 years to his wife, Grace, and continues to marvel at her incredible patience in putting up with him and his computer illiteracy.

At the moment, he is currently at work on his tenth Sherlock Holmes novel.

Keep reading for an excerpt from Richard T. Ryan's next book:

The Other Woman:

A Sherlock Holmes Adventure

(a working title)

by Richard Ryan

Chapter One

Sherlock Holmes returned late one August afternoon, and upon entering our flat and seeing me sitting at my desk, stated. "Watson, I have just had a most singular experience."

For anything to make such an impression upon the usually unflappable Holmes was indeed noteworthy. "Do tell, old man," I encouraged him.

"I had just emerged from my bolt hole in the Shadwell section of the East End where I had followed one of the suspects in the recent theft of the Gough Map from the Bodelian Library. As I am sure you know, the Gough Map, one of the earliest maps of Britain, is a national treasure and as such it's priceless."

Actually I didn't but I always hated confessing my ignorance to Holmes, so I replied, "Really, I hadn't heard anything about it."

"I should hope not. The university trustees have spent a great deal of money to cover up the theft, and rather than involve the police, they have tasked me with recovering the map as well as the other stolen documents. In the meantime, at my suggestion, they are updating their security systems throughout the various buildings."

"I don't understand. If the theft occurred in Oxford, why are you following a man here in London?"

"Because I am certain he was involved. Everett Majors is no ordinary thief. After attending the Royal Military College at Sandhurst, he spent several years in the army serving with distinction in Ireland with the 1st Dragoons. However, like so many others he found the lure of easy money too tempting to resist and resigned his commission before scandal overtook him.

"As a result of his training, he is a master planner. Were the Professor still alive, I am certain he would have taken Majors in hand and developed his skills even further. However, I digress. After learning where Majors lived, I set a team of my Irregulars to watch him. Today, I decided to check in on him myself. After several hours during which he never left his rooms, I decided to doff my disguise, change into my frock coat and collar, and return here to pass the time in more pleasant surroundings. The youngsters have been instructed to notify me should Majors receive any visitors or leave his flat.

"As I boarded an omnibus, I noticed a young man clamber aboard at the last minute. He was slightly built and wearing a rather distinctive double-breasted waistcoat and a wheel cap that seemed incongruous."

"So far I fail to see anything even slightly unusual, let alone singular, about your experience," I remarked.

"I'm getting to the point," he said as he charged his pipe. "Once or twice during the trip, I looked up from the paper I was pretending to read and thought I caught the young man glancing at me. With my suspicions now aroused, I decided to disembark from the bus at Regent's Park and walk home from there. I was quite relieved when I descended and watched the bus pull away with the young man still aboard.

"So imagine my surprise when I turned onto Baker Street and saw the same fellow loitering in front of a store across the street and pretending to study the contents of the shop windows."

"Did you approach him?"

"No, I walked past him and continued to Melcombe Street where I turned and made my way to the alley which runs parallel to Baker Street. I entered through the rear – oh, by the way, Mrs. Hudson is making curried mutton for dinner – and then ran up here so that I might watch him unobserved from the front window."

While he was speaking, Holmes was charging his pipe and lighting it. Having said all this, he then took up a position perhaps two or three feet from the window so he could see without being seen.

"Is he still there?" I asked.

All of a sudden I heard Holmes laugh and then more to himself than me, he said, "Of all the unbridled cheek."

"Holmes, what happened?"

"The young man just looked up the window, saluted me and then sauntered off down Baker Street as though he hadn't a care in the world."

"Do you have any idea what it means?"

"None whatsoever, but you may be certain I intend to find out."

For the next several days, Holmes divided his efforts between keeping a watchful eye on Majors and in his spare time attempting to track down the young fellow. I knew with him it was a matter of pride. Although he had hardly been "defeated," a word he chose to apply to the encounter, I knew he felt he had been bested in some way – and the list of people that could lay claim to having done that was a remarkably short one. In fact he had once admitted to being beaten four times – "three times by men and once by a woman."

I couldn't see where this was anything more than a mere trifle but then I recalled his telling me on more than one occasion, "There is nothing so important as trifles."

Finally, several days later, Holmes entered the flat perhaps 30 minutes before dinner. He said nothing, but I could tell that he was vexed. After lighting his pipe and settling into his chair, he looked at me and said, "I must admit to being at a loss, Watson. I have searched everywhere from here to Shadwell, but no one has seen the young man I am seeking."

"I think you are making entirely too much out of this," I said. "You believe that you were followed on one occasion by a man you have not seen since, nor has your vast network of informants been able to discover his whereabouts – much less his identity. Perhaps he was simply an admirer. Is it not possible that you are mistaken?"

Holmes gave me a withering glance before he said, "No, Watson, I am not in error. Had you seen the insouciant manner in which he waved at me as he walked away, I am certain you would agree. It was as though he were saying, 'This round to me, Mr. Holmes.'"

The next morning as we were eating breakfast, Holmes was busy reading his letters from the first post of the day. He would finish one and then either drop it on the floor to be collected later and burned – a fate shared by the vast majority of his letters. Occasionally, he would read one a second time before disposing of it. Rarely, would he give a letter a third read, and on those occasions, he would place it on the table for future reference. On this morning, such was the case with the very last letter that he read.

I watched with fascination as Holmes perused the missive – thrice. Finally, he handed it to me and said, "Watson, what do you make of this?"

I took the letter and read it.

Dear Mr. Holmes,

If you are free, I shall call upon you this afternoon at half past three. If that time is inconvenient, I beg you to write me and suggest a more auspicious time.

I am contacting you on a matter of some urgency. I believe I can trust you as you did right by my sister several years ago.

If I do not hear from you, I shall see you later today.

Sincerely yours,

Serena Erne

Determined to apply the methods I had observed my friend employ on so many occasions, I began by stating, "Judging by the quality of the paper, I think it is safe to assume your correspondent must be well-off."

Holmes said nothing but nodded.

"It was written by a woman, surely, one who has been tutored – no doubt by an accomplished governess – and as a result is no doubt quite accomplished herself."

"Excellent," continued Holmes. "Continue, I pray you."

Having warmed to my task and bolstered by Holmes's praise, I carried on, "The script reflects a strong personality and her choice of words and syntax would all seem to reinforce my deductions. She may even be a noblewoman." I paused, looked at my friend and asked, "How did I do?"

"Well, I agree that it was written by a woman and she may indeed but well off, but I don't think the paper offers any insight into that. In fact, I shouldn't be surprised if the paper were provided by the hotel in which she is presently residing.

"As for her being schooled by a proper governess, I am inclined to think she is American."

"American?"

"You mentioned syntax – when I see 'half past three' instead of the more common 'half three' followed by 'I beg you to write me' rather than 'to write *to* me' and shortly after we see the very colloquial 'I shall see you later today'' rather than the more formal 'I shall call upon you' – I think we can safely dispense with the notion of a British governess and turn our sights towards the former Colonies.''

I was too dumbfounded to replay. When I said nothing, Holmes asked, "Was there nothing else that struck you?"

Having embarrassed myself enough, I said, "Why don't you just tell me what else I missed?"

"It's not that you missed anything, but I must admit the name is rather suggestive."

"By the way, do you recall her sister?"

"No, in fact, I am quite certain I never handled a case for a woman with the last name of Erne."

"That may be the correspondent's married name," I suggested, "or perhaps her sister was wed and had a different surname when you assisted her."

"That is certainly a possibility," replied Holmes, "but I am inclined to view things from a slightly different perspective." He then turned and withdrew one of his yearbooks from the shelves without elaborating any further.

Feeling both chagrined and relieved that the letter was now behind us, I decided not to press my friend on the issue and just wait and see what the afternoon brought.

The morning passed slowly and after lunch I was so immersed in detailing the case of the Pernicious Publican that I was quite startled to hear the bell ring. I glanced at my watch and saw that it was exactly half three. "If nothing else, this woman is certainly punctual," I thought. And it was just a moment later that our landlady knocked on the door and Holmes bade her enter.

"A young woman to see you, Mr. Holmes," said Mrs. Hudson. "She said her name is Serena Erne and she has an appointment."

"Indeed, she does, Mr. Hudson. Would be so kind as to show her up and perhaps put on the kettle?"

"Indeed, Mr. Holmes," she replied.

No sooner had she departed than a woman tapped on the door. She was dressed all in black, and I immediately assumed from her garb and the veil she was wearing that she was still grieving the loss of someone close. Holmes and I both rose, and he said, "Do come in. I am Sherlock Holmes, and this is my colleague and friend, Dr. John Watson."

Although I could not see her face, she moved gracefully, suggesting she was younger rather than older.

She was tall and slender. But beyond that I could deduce little else.

She took the seat indicated by Holmes who then spoke to her saying, "In your letter you said that I was of some assistance to your sister; unfortunately, I cannot recall a client with the surname of Erne."

"That was not my sister's surname. Erne is my husband's name," she replied.

Although her diction was perfect and she had obviously studied elocution, there was no doubt from her speech she was American.

"Well that certainly explains the confusion," I offered, smiling at her before I caught Holmes grinning at me.

Holmes then picked up the conversation. "If you would be so kind as to tell me your sister's name."

"It is not important," said our visitor. "She passed away several months ago."

"Still, for my own edification," insisted Holmes. "You never know; perhaps she will have some bearing on the issue which has brought you hither."

"I fail to see how that could be possible," she replied.

At that moment, Mrs. Hudson knocked on the door. "Here is the tea you requested, Mr. Holmes. I've also brought up a basket with some blueberry muffins which I baked this morning."

"Thank you, Mrs. Hudson," he said. Then turning to our visitor, he asked, "Perhaps you would care for some tea or a muffin, Mrs. Erne?"

I suspected the tea was a ploy to get the woman to raise her veil. I'm certain Holmes was hoping that he might discern a family resemblance.

However, she declined the tea, and I could see a hint of frustration flit across my friend's face. However, he quickly recovered his composure and turning to our visitor, he asked, "Well then let us begin at the beginning and why don't you tell us what has brought you to Baker Street, Miss Adler?"

www.ingramcontent.com/pod-product-compliance
Lightning Source LLC
Chambersburg PA
CBHW020235260626
47156CB00002B/687